FACE OF A STRANGER

After five years, Alison realised that her marriage was in trouble. To fund yet another of his business ventures, her husband, Alec, had pawned her most treasured possession — a gold bracelet she had inherited from her grandmother — and then he had disappeared. When Alison turns to the parents of her best friend, Judy, for comfort, they tell her that Alec has been killed. Alison then tries to get in touch with Judy — but why is she always unavailable?

JANE CARRICK

FACE OF A STRANGER

Complete and Unabridged

LINFORD
Leicester

First published in Great Britain in 1980

First Linford Edition
published 2004

British Library CIP Data

Carrick, Jane
    Face of a stranger.—Large print ed.—
Linford romance library
    1. Love stories
    2. Large type books
    I. Title
    823.9'14 [F]

    ISBN 1–84395–119–3

Published by
F. A. Thorpe (Publishing)
Anstey, Leicestershire

Set by Words & Graphics Ltd.
Anstey, Leicestershire
Printed and bound in Great Britain by
T. J. International Ltd., Padstow, Cornwall

This book is printed on acid-free paper

Who Was To Blame?

Alison Drummond leaned over her drawing-board, her eyes smarting with concentration as she used her finest sable brush on the eye of a hawfinch. Under her skilful fingers, the beautiful bird slowly came to life, and she sat back with a contented sigh.

She had been commissioned to do a series of bird paintings for a new book, and the hawfinch represented the last in the series.

Alison wiped her hands on a rag and glanced at the time, wondering where Alec had gone. The light was beginning to fade now from their Edinburgh flat, usually so bright and airy in the daytime.

This evening it seemed oppressive, however, as Alison gazed down on the wet streets, thronged with people going about their business. For most of them

1

there was a sense of purpose in their movements, but a few wandered about aimlessly. Were they unemployed, like Alec, she wondered.

Then she remembered with a wry smile that Alec was never unemployed. He was always merely 'between projects.' She slid off her stool and walked into the kitchen to plug in the electric kettle.

It was five years now since she and Alec had married. How happy she had been, at nineteen, she thought wistfully.

Meeting Alec had gone a long way to helping Alison recover from the untimely death of her parents, who had been killed in a motoring accident. Her father had been in the Diplomatic Service and they'd been abroad when the accident had ocurred.

In her romantic haze, it would have been all too easy to give up her place at art school. In fact, Alec had actively encouraged her to do just that.

'Come on, Alison,' he'd said. 'What's the point in slogging away at that dreary old place when you don't have to?' He'd smiled at her then.

'I'm going to set up a small motor accessory business with that windfall my Uncle Alexander left me. It'll be a wee goldmine, so why don't you just concentrate on being a full-time wife?'

But Alison had been adamant about finishing her course. She'd promised her mother that she would — and that promise meant a lot to her now.

All the same, at times like these she missed the sound, down-to-earth advice her parents always gave her.

Still, she always had Judy to turn to . . .

Alison and Judy Millar had been friends since they were children, and if Alison's artistic temperament sometimes made her impulsive, Judy's sound commonsense was usually a calming influence.

But nothing had stopped Alison from marrying Alec Drummond, with Judy as bridesmaid, and a small gathering of family and friends to wish them well.

Alec had no relatives, having just lost his uncle and guardian, but he had a number of friends, whose noisy antics at the reception had raised a few eyebrows!

It was just as well Alison had stayed on at art school. Alec's ventures into the business world had always been fraught with disasters, none of which was of his own making — at least as far as he was concerned.

Often, too, there were debts to pay and Alison had had to settle his accounts, even as he enthusiastically outlined a new idea which was to be a sure-fire success.

Alison had inherited all the pretty jewellery that her mother had loved to wear, and the girl often thought how sad she would have been if she had known it had all been sold to pay Alec's debts — with the sole exception of the beautiful gem-set gold bracelet that had belonged to her grandmother.

Alison steadfastly refused to part with this. Some day she might have a daughter of her own, who would treasure this family heirloom.

Some day, surely, Alec would really grow up and begin to accept his responsibilities. Only then could they settle down as a family and begin to build a good life.

If only Alec would help out a little more in the flat while he was between projects! But he declared himself to be an absolute moron in the kitchen, and couldn't — or wouldn't — even boil an egg.

Alison put the vegetables in the pressure cooker and decided to open a tin of corned beef. It wasn't going to be one of Alec's favourite meals, but she was in no mood now to prepare anything more elaborate.

She set the small table in the kitchen, then, as an afterthought, she added two pretty candles with matching napkins.

The pressure cooker was hissing gently when she heard Alec's footsteps on the stairs, and a moment later he came bounding into the flat, whistling cheerfully.

Alison hardly knew whether to be elated or worried to death. She knew all the signs. Alec was about to make a fortune with some new scheme!

'Hello, love!' he called cheerfully. 'Guess where I've been!'

'Oh, I'm no good at guessing games,' Alison said tiredly. 'Come on through, Alec. The vegetables are just cooked. It's corned beef . . . '

'Couldn't be better,' Alec said happily as he came into the kitchen. He moved over to her and planted a kiss on her cheek. He looked young and boyish with a wisp of fair hair falling into his eyes.

'I hope there's something nice for pud,' he said, rubbing his hands.

'Lemon pie?' Alison replied, teasing him. She knew he loved lemon pie.

'Great!' He enfolded her in a bear hug. 'Didn't you miss me today?' Alison shook her head and wriggled free.

'Well, I've been away all afternoon,'

he said huffily. 'And you've got such a one-track mind about all that art work of yours!'

'That's what pays the bills,' Alison said quietly.

'Don't you worry, darling. I'll be paying the bills soon. I'll be making enough money to pay most of them in advance if I want. Ken says so . . . '

'Ken?'

'Ken Doig. Surely you know Ken?'

Alison sat back, her appetite deserting her. 'Of course I do! I've known him since I was five!'

'Well, you know what a marvellous business he's built up — stationery, gifts, that sort of stuff. Well, he wants to expand, to get into the city centre. And he's willing to take me on as a partner.' Alec paused.

★ ★ ★

Alison stared at him disbelievingly. She, Ken and Judy had all been at school together. While she had excelled in art,

Ken and Judy had always rivalled one another for the top grades in maths and science.

Judy had graduated with a First Class Honours degree in chemistry, and Ken had gradually developed a very astute business brain.

Alison could understand Ken's desire to expand, but he must surely know Alec's business record.

'A partner!' she exclaimed. 'What sort of partner?'

'He hasn't worked out the details yet,' Alec replied, avoiding her eyes. 'But I'd need a lump sum, Alison — to put into the business, you understand . . . '

'I understand only too well,' Alison said under her breath.

She had no doubt that whatever Ken offered Alec, it would be a very fair deal, and a few years ago she would have had no hesitation. But not now — not again. And this time not just for Alec's sake, but for Ken's as well.

Alison's cheeks flamed now as she

realised what he was doing for her. He must be well aware of Alec's incompetence, yet he was willing to risk that in an effort to help them.

'You know nothing about Ken's business, Alec,' she said quietly.

'You said that about the filling station,' he replied quickly. 'But I soon got the hang of it, didn't I?'

'Not enough to make it pay!'

'That wasn't my fault!' Alec cried. 'I wasn't responsible for the price of oil going up! But it'll be different this time. This time Ken will be able to foresee all the snags.'

Perhaps that's true, Alison thought, but if Ken Doig was going to expand, he needed someone who would work as hard as he did himself, and Alison knew Alec was incapable of sustained hard work.

'We can afford it, can't we?' Alec asked aggressively. 'You're always getting big cheques . . .'

'We need every penny I earn,' Alison snapped. Her mind went to the extra account she had opened, without telling Alec about it — the account which was her insurance against the times when there was no work coming in for her.

'Surely you're going to help me!' Alec demanded.

'No!' she replied firmly. 'We can't afford it. This time I can't help you.'

He stared at her disbelievingly. 'But — but, Alison!'

'No, Alec, I mean it.'

'But we can't pass up a chance like this! How can I fail with Ken behind me?' His eyes filled with angry frustration.

He stood up, his young face colouring with anger. Then he turned from her and snatched up his coat.

'Where are you going?' she asked him.

'Out! It doesn't matter where I'm going!'

A moment later, the door slammed, and Alison wearily began to tidy up the supper dishes. Had she done the right thing?

★ ★ ★

Alison was already in bed when Alec came home late that night, but she pretended to be asleep when she heard the persuasive note in his voice as he whispered her name. Being left alone to think things out had only strengthened her resolution.

Next morning, she got out of bed early and had already cleaned the flat and laid the table for Alec's breakfast before he appeared from the bedroom.

Alison was wearing her outdoor clothing, and Alec stared at her sulkily.

'Going out?' he asked.

'I have to go to Ian Thomson's for some new brushes,' she said evenly. 'I'll get something for lunch while I'm out.'

'Oh, don't put yourself out for my sake!' he flung at her. 'Since I'm such a burden to you, I'll manage with a sandwich. You make life difficult for yourself, Alison. If you'd only co-operate . . . '

Alison had slept badly, unsure about

whether or not she was doing the right thing. Now she felt she just couldn't take any more.

'Co-operate!' she cried. 'When have I not been asked to co-operate? How many times have I bailed you out, and how often have you let me down?'

Suddenly she and Alec were quarreling with a fierce and bitter anger. She thought about the hard-earned money he had wasted, and the jewellery and ornaments that had had to be sold.

She listened to his blustering excuses, and her mind seemed to become razor sharp and ruthless as she cut them down. Then, equally quickly, the anger drained out of her.

'I can't argue all day, Alec. I have my work to do. If you really want to make a success of your life, then forget about beginning at the top. I'd suggest a visit to the Job Centre.' She picked up her bag and rushed out of the flat.

Normally the short walk to Ian Thomson's where she bought her art materials calmed her down, but this morning her face was white and set as she swung open the door of his small shop.

Ian Thomson looked up as the old doorbell clanged vigorously. Someone, he decided, must be in rather a hurry. He came through from the back of the shop and his rather serious face broke into a smile when he saw Alison.

Over the years, since he had inherited the shop from his father, Ian had taken a keen interest in his customers. He loved paintings and always regretted that he had no talent in that direction himself, but he was well content with his life.

Alison Drummond often came into the shop, her eyes full of excitement as she told him about the latest commission.

One day, however, when she had half-jokingly said he was the only one who really appreciated her success, he'd begun to suspect that her marriage wasn't going all that smoothly.

This morning Alison looked more

upset than Ian had ever seen her, though she tried to smile.

'You'll wonder what I do with all my small sable brushes, Ian,' she said. 'You'll be thinking I eat them! Anyway, this time I'm after size numbers two to four. Oh, and I'd like a tube of . . . '

She saw he was staring at her anxiously and she tried to wipe the tears away, but a moment later Ian had closed the shop door and turned the sign.

'I think we could both do with a cup of coffee, don't you?' he said. 'Come on through and I'll put the kettle on.'

It's nice having my decisions made for me for a change, Alison thought, as she allowed Ian to lead her through to the small living-room at the back of the shop. As she sat down, she could no longer stem the flood of tears. She got out a handkerchief and held it over her face in both hands.

Ian waited for her sobs to subside, then handed her a mug of coffee.

'Sorry,' she said uncertainly, and

sipped the warm drink. 'Thanks, Ian.'

His solemn face was etched with concern for her, and he wanted to shoulder every burden Alison possessed. He looked down on her bowed head, longing to put comforting arms around her. How often in the past had he felt an almost overwhelming anger against Alec Drummond?

Ian lowered his tall, lean frame on to a wooden chair. 'How can I help?' he asked gently.

'There's nothing you can do, Ian.' Alison smiled through her tears. 'You've been a great help as it is.'

'Is it Alec?' He probed hesitantly.

She nodded. 'He — he's been given another chance, Ian,' she replied. 'It means putting up capital again, though, and this time I'm not going to do it.'

'Good for you!' Ian said. 'It's time he did something for himself, Alison. He might not make so many mistakes if you don't keep rushing to his aid.'

'But I'm not sure if I've done the right thing,' she said miserably.

'If you ask me, you should have made a stand years ago,' Ian said.

Alison felt better after she left Ian's shop with all her supplies. Swiftly she walked along to the supermarket, searching in her pocket for her shopping list, and soon she was wandering around, picking up items and comparing prices.

Her arms ached, however, when she finally returned to the flat, letting herself in with her key. She made a cup of tea and for a few moments relaxed in her favourite kitchen chair. Then, with a sigh, she crossed the landing to her bedroom.

As she picked up the brush to tidy her hair, her gaze fell on the square envelope propped against the dressing-table mirror. Slowly she picked it up and took out the letter inside.

Alison darling, she read, I'm leaving you . . . Her hand shook and her legs turned to jelly as she sat down. I know you're wrong about Ken's offer, and you'll realise that yourself sooner or later, but by that time it may be too late for me, and Ken might have taken on someone else.

So I'm making my own decision over this, and you needn't worry about ready cash, because I know a jeweller and pawnbroker who's willing to lend on your grandmother's antique gold bracelet . . .

Alison's face went white. He had taken her one really good piece of jewellery, her grandmother's bracelet.

It's really quite valuable, Alec had written, though I know it only has sentimental value for you. It might not raise all I need, but it will be enough for now.

I consider this a temporary loan, as I'll be able to get it back for you very soon. And I'll be able to afford a ring to match.

This time I intend to be a success, but you just hold me back, so I'll do it my way for a change.

I'll be in touch — Alec.

Alison read and re-read the note,

waves of weariness washing over her.

If only her parents were here — or Judy . . .

Judy now lived in London, where she worked in a research laboratory. Alison went to the telephone and dialled Judy's number. She could hear it ringing repeatedly, then she put down the receiver, feeling impatient with herself. Of course, Judy wouldn't be home yet!

As the afternoon dragged on, she made another attempt to reach Judy. But as she sat at her desk, her eyes fell on the calendar and she realised that Judy could not be in London. She would be at Calderlea.

★　★　★

Calderlea was the village near Perth where the Millar family lived. It had been Alison's home almost as much as Judy's. Mr and Mrs Millar had been almost as dear to her own parents, and Judy was just like a sister.

On a sudden impulse, Alison began to throw clothes into a suitcase. Judy always went home at this time of year for a break before winter set in. No doubt she would have been ringing Alison any day now, asking her to come up to Calderlea for a couple of days.

For several years Alec had gone with her, but last year he'd said he was bored with Calderlea and had remained in Edinburgh.

Alison picked up her suitcase and went round the flat, making sure that no switch had been left on, and that everything was secure. Ian Thomson would look after things for her, she was sure of that, and he could forward any mail to Calderlea.

Alison was thinking about Ian as she drove towards the Forth Bridge, in her white Mini.

'Just what the doctor ordered,' he'd said when she'd told him her plans. 'Just you stay away as long as you like, Alison. I'll be happy to see to things for you, and if Alec decides to come home . . . '

'He won't,' she'd said, her voice bleak. 'I know Alec. He'll be enjoying his new-found freedom, and — and he won't need me just yet.'

'It'll do him good to stand on his own two feet for a while,' Ian said briskly, though inwardly he was trembling with anger for her. 'This might be the best possible thing, Alison.'

'Yes.' She nodded. Perhaps Alec would make a go of things this time.

But now she was conscious of a strange sense of relief as she drove towards Calderlea. It was like going home once more, and tonight she would be sleeping in the old-fashioned comfortable bed.

Sometimes she and Judy had talked and laughed into the early hours until reminded by angry thumps from Mrs Millar's walking-stick from below that it was long past their bedtime.

Hillside was about half a mile beyond the church and the school in Calderlea, and Alison could see the sitting-room lights blazing as she drove through the wrought-iron gates.

The curtain moved and Beth Millar's wispy grey hair was outlined. Alison waved as she got out of the car and the face disappeared from the window. A moment later, the front door opened and Mrs Millar was there, holding out her arms to her.

'Alison!' she cried. 'How nice to see you!' She clasped Alison warmly in her arms then escorted her into the sitting-room, where Mr Millar got up from his armchair.

'Isn't Judy here?' Alison asked.

She heard Mrs Millar catch her breath a little.

'Judy?' she asked brightly. 'Why — why no, dear. She isn't here just now.'

Alison felt slightly taken aback. 'I thought she always came home at this time of year,' she said.

'Yes, well, not just at the moment, Alison.'

'Are you having a wee holiday to yourself?' Mr Millar asked. 'And what's the idea of bringing all this food? Were you expecting Mother and I to starve you?' He looked at her quizzically, expecting her to laugh, but suddenly Alison was sobbing helplessly, while Mrs Millar led her to the settee.

'Put the box in the kitchen, Walter dear,' she said over her shoulder. 'Alison's case can go in her room. Now, dear, suppose you tell me what it's all about.'

★　★　★

Long after Alison was in bed, she could still hear the low murmur of Mr and Mrs Millar's voices as they talked together.

It had been easy, after a while, to tell both Mr and Mrs Millar about Alec, and about the years which had gone before. She knew they hadn't been entirely unaware of what she had been going through, and now Mrs Millar could see that Alison had reached a crossroads in her marriage.

'You did the right thing, coming to us, darling,' she said gently. 'Your wee room is always ready, just — just like Judy's . . . ' Her voice had faltered suspiciously at that point, but a moment later she continued firmly. 'You can stay here just as long as you like. It will do us all good, I'm sure.'

'It will certainly do you good, love,' Mr Millar said, looking at his wife.

'You don't have enough to do these days while I'm at work.'

'I don't have enough to do!' his wife cried. 'Have you seen your green pullover recently? It has no elbows in it at all!'

They bickered amicably, but Alison could see beyond their outward light-heartedness to the concern in their eyes for her.

It seemed to colour the whole atmosphere in the house, she thought, almost as though she had brought her tension along with her. It seemed she couldn't escape from her doubts and fears, not even at Calderlea.

During the next few days, Alison began to feel more like herself as she helped Mrs Millar in the house, and swept up leaves in the garden, giving Mr Millar a hand to put them on to a huge bonfire.

They're getting older, she thought, as she watched Judy's parents going about their everyday tasks. At one time they had both been full of fun and energy, but Mr and Mrs Millar had now grown a great deal quieter.

If only Judy were here, Alison thought. But Judy seemed to have made other plans for her autumn break, and if her parents knew about them, they had decided to keep them to themselves.

Once or twice she had tried to talk to Mrs Millar, but the older woman's face had coloured a little and she had skilfully changed the subject. At first Alison had wondered if Judy had quarrelled with her parents, even though that seemed unthinkable.

Then, as though off-guard, they had talked about her one morning over breakfast, and all the love and pride the Millars felt for their only daughter was obvious in the warmth of their voices.

Mrs Millar's eyes had actually filled with tears, but she simply parried Alison's concerned remarks.

Alison said nothing, but as the time passed she grew more and more convinced that something was wrong. She and Judy had always seemed to know when anything was seriously wrong with the other.

She remembered once, as schoolgirls, that they had gone to visit friends of Mrs Millar's who owned a farm. Alison had loved to look at the hens and chicks while Judy preferred to romp through the fields.

When Judy had been late for tea, her mother hadn't been unduly worried since Judy had little sense of time. Alison, however, had a strange sense of unease and had persuaded everyone to look for Judy straightaway. She had been found clinging to the broken branch of a tree, in the swirling river.

Alison and Judy had had this affinity with one another, and sometimes they had been teased about it by Ken Doig, who went to the same school in Edinburgh.

Later, Judy's parents had moved to Perth, and they had kept an eye on Alison while her parents were abroad. That way, Alison's schooling had been uninterrupted.

Now, however, in spite of her worries, she was beginning to feel rested once again in the Millar household.

'Is there anything I can do for you today?' she asked Mrs Millar.

'Well, if you really want to help you could polish the brasses and silver.'

'Sure — I'd enjoy that,' Alison replied with a smile.

★ ★ ★

She was just starting on a pair of old candlesticks when a car turned into the

26

drive, and she glanced out of the window. Her heart leapt as the tall figure of Ken Doig climbed from the driving seat.

'It's Ken,' she said to Mrs Millar. 'What on earth does he want?'

The older woman paused for a moment, then hurried to the door.

'Is Alison here, Mrs Millar?' he asked. 'I — I've got to see her rather urgently.'

Alison rose to her feet as Mrs Millar ushered Ken into the living-room. Why had he followed her here?

'How did you know where to find me?' she asked curiously.

'Ian Thomson told me. Look, I'm sorry, Alison I — I hardly know how to tell you . . . ' He looked anxiously from Mrs Millar to Alison, his eyes full of distress.

Then Alison stepped forward. 'Just tell me,' she said quietly.

'There's been an accident. It's Alec,' Ken said hoarsely. 'I'm sorry, love, but he — he's dead. He was doing some work for me, you know, on my expansion plans, and I — I allowed him to use my car.'

Distressed, Ken went on — 'He had to go to Manchester to look at some new lines which we might be able to use. Anyway, the road must have been unfamiliar to him . . . He was killed outright, Alison.'

Alison was only dimly aware of Mrs Millar pushing her into a chair by the fireside, and Ken sitting down beside her and taking her hand in his.

'It's largely my fault,' Ken was saying. 'I asked him to go. I let him have my car, and . . . '

'From what you say, it was an accident,' Mrs Millar said, as she handed both of them a hot drink. 'So stop blaming yourself, Ken. All the same, it's a tragedy and no mistake. Alec was such a young man. I — I'll go and ring Walter.'

Alison had begun to sob, the tears coursing down her cheeks, while Ken held her hands.

'Let her have a good cry,' Mrs Millar said. 'It's better to come out.'

The next few days seemed to be a living nightmare for Alison. She returned to Edinburgh to make the funeral arrangements. The flat had a strange effect on her and seemed to chill her heart even though Mrs Millar had insisted on accompanying her.

Somehow the place still seemed to be full of Alec's presence and she could almost hear his voice echoing from every corner.

Mrs Millar looked at the girl's stricken face.

'We'll go back to Calderlea after the funeral, dear,' she said gently. 'I'll help you to leave the flat in good order, but you mustn't stay here by yourself. You'll only start blaming yourself again.'

Alison nodded, though she found it difficult, deep down, not to blame herself. The thought that she could have helped Alec if she had wanted to would always be with her.

If she and Alec had still been living in

29

the flat, it would have just been like all the other jobs to Alec. After a while he would have settled into some sort of routine and this time Ken would have been around to keep an eye on him. This time it just might have worked . . .

It was a week or two before Alison began to walk around Calderlea again. She loved Perthshire, especially in the autumn of the year when the seasonal tints lit up the countryside.

The local people had all expressed their sympathy to Alison for her loss, and now they began to greet her cheerfully, and to encourage her to take part in local affairs.

It occurred to her that Mrs Millar hadn't been going out much recently to her usual Women's Fellowship meetings, or to the Women's Institute.

'I hope you aren't staying at home because of me,' Alison said one day. 'I feel I've put you out enough already.'

'Nonsense!' Mrs Millar said. 'You don't know how plesed I am to have you, Alison. And you're a great help, running errands and so on.' A sudden thought stuck her. 'That reminds me, could you pop down to the general stores and see if Elsie Ross has any glycerine? I want to ice a cake and I used the last lot to preserve those beech leaves.'

'I'll go straightaway,' Alison said, reaching into the hall cupboard for her anorak.

It was a lovely, crisp morning, and her cheeks were beginning to show a little more colour.

It was nearly a quarter of a mile to the shop, and Alison stood aside to allow a shiny, black car to pass, but instead it slowly rolled to a stop, and the window was wound down.

'Hello, Alison.'

★　★　★

As Alison stared into the car, her face lit up with pleasure when she recognised Blair Walker, Judy's fiancé.

'Well, how lovely to see you, Blair!'

she exclaimed. 'Have you just come home?'

He nodded. 'I've been working in Aberdeen, as I expect you know.'

'You geologists get about,' Alison said. 'Mind you, I don't know how you and Judy keep the romance going with each of you at opposite ends of the country!'

Blair's usual answering smile was absent, however, and Alison looked down at him closely.

He was a broad, stocky, young man with wiry, brown hair and grey eyes. His slightly-snub nose gave him a cheerful look, even when he was being serious.

He and Judy were the best of friends, as well as being in love with one another, Alison had always envied them that, she remembered, and her eyes shadowed.

She and Alec had loved one another, that was true, but they hadn't always been good friends.

'Can I give you a lift?' Blair asked.

'No, I'm walking for the good of my health. You — you heard about Alec?'

'Yes, I'm sorry, Alison — more sorry than I can say.' He looked at her keenly, seeing the grief in her eyes. 'It was a tragedy, Alison. He had his whole life in front of him.'

'I know,' she said huskily. It still hurt to talk about Alec to someone who knew them both well.

'At least, you're in the best place to help you get over it, Alison. Are you sure I can't give you a lift?'

'Oh, all right,' Alison said, slipping into the passenger seat.

'I don't suppose Judy is home?' Blair asked.

Alison stared at him in surprise. She felt that Blair was almost holding his breath, waiting for her answer.

'Why no, Blair,' she said. 'You mean you — you don't know where she is?'

Slowly he shook his head. Instead of driving on, he reached into his pocket and produced a letter.

'Read that,' he invited.

She turned the letter over, recognising Judy's large scrawl on the envelope.

'But — but it's addressed to you, Blair, and . . . '

'Read it,' Blair repeated firmly.

Slowly Alison pulled out the single sheet of paper. There was no address on it, and Judy had wasted few words. It was a gentle enough letter, but it left Blair in no doubt that their engagement was at an end.

'What am I supposed to make of that, Alison?' he asked.

She swallowed, reading the words slowly again as though trying to find a clue to their meaning.

'I — I just don't know, Blair,' she said helplessly. 'Judy hasn't written to me for ages, but that didn't worry me. Neither of us needs to write often, if you know what I mean.'

Then her expression clouded.

'She did send a wreath for Alec, though. I've tried to talk to Mrs Millar once or twice, but she doesn't seem to want to say much either.'

She handed the letter back to him.

'I was even beginning to wonder if Judy was on some special hush-hush project, Blair. But this letter only makes me more confused than ever — I just don't know what to think.'

'Neither do I,' he said grimly. 'I went to her flat, but she's left there, and she doesn't seem to be at the research laboratory either. I suppose she could have met someone else,' he added jealously.

'Oh, no!' A look of amazement spread over Alison's face.

'Why not? She's a — a very beautiful girl, you know, Alison.'

'But she wouldn't let you down like this.'

'She might not want to get caught up in any argument — and I *would* argue. Judy knows I'd fight for her.'

Alison nodded. Her first instinct had been to rush home and confront the Millars with Blair's news, but now she felt it might be wiser to say nothing for the moment.

'Will you see her parents?' she asked in a low voice.

'I don't feel like seeing anyone just yet,' Blair told her. 'I just wondered if you knew anything. I had to ask, Alison.'

'I don't know anything,' she told him. 'It's a terrible state of affairs, I must say. What are you going to do, Blair?'

'Well, nothing at the moment. I've got to be back in Aberdeen tomorrow. Oh, and Alison, I'd appreciate it if you'd keep all this to yourself for the moment.'

She nodded, and a faint smile reached her eyes. 'Don't worry, I won't be telling Elsie Ross!'

For once Alison was on her own that evening. Mr and Mrs Millar had gone to visit an old friend in Perth and she had assured them that she would be perfectly happy to mind the house.

'Well, I've made up some sandwiches and there's cake in the tins,' Mrs Millar said. 'Don't forget to make yourself some supper, Alison. You're still as thin as a rake.'

'If you fatten me up any more, my clothes won't fit me!' Alison joked. She had bought wool and a pattern at the shop and she had decided to knit a winter cardigan for Mrs Millar.

She read the complicated pattern aloud as she knitted the first row, then she put the work down with a small exclamation of impatience as the telephone shrilled loudly.

'What a nuisance!' she muttered aloud. 'Who can that be?'

A moment later her heart was beating wildly with delight when she recognised Judy's voice.

'Hello, Mum?'

'Judy! Oh, Judy. It's me — Alison! Oh, it's great to hear from you! Where are you?'

There was a short silence, while Alison heard Judy catch her breath.

'I'm sorry, Alison, but I — I can't talk to you,' she said clearly. 'I want to talk to my mother.'

No Resemblance!

Alison's hand trembled and she felt stunned as she put down the telephone receiver. Judy had actually hung up on her after Alison had told her Mr and Mrs Millar were out for the evening!

How could Judy do a thing like that to her, Alison wondered, especially when she needed her so badly at this time? Losing Alec had left a deep, painful wound which she felt would never heal. A few words of sympathy from her dearest friend would have helped so much.

Slowly, Alison picked up her knitting again, then thrust it aside. She would only make mistakes. She forgot about the supper Mrs Millar had prepared for her, and forgot to keep the fire banked up, so that the room was cold when Mr and Mrs Millar returned home.

Alison had kept the television on,

using it only as background for her thoughts, but now she jumped up to switch it off, and turned with an exclamation of dismay when she realised they had returned.

'Oh, I'm sorry,' she said contritely. 'I — I forgot about the fire . . . '

'You forgot to eat your supper, too,' Mrs Millar scolded mildly, as she walked through to the kitchen. 'It's just as I left it, Alison.'

She came back and looked more closely at the girl's pale face.

'What's wrong, Alison?' she asked. 'Has something happened?'

Hearing the kindness and concern in Mrs Millar's voice, Alison had to fight back the tears.

'It — it was Judy,' she said huskily. 'She was on the telephone asking for you. When I told her you were out she said she'd phone back later. She wouldn't speak to me.'

Mr and Mrs Millar exchanged glances, and it seemed to Alison that a wordless message had flashed between them. There seemed to be a high wall between her and the Millars, and Alison felt afraid of something which she didn't understand.

'Oh, my dear, I'm sorry,' Mrs Millar said. 'What a pity we weren't in.' It was obvious that she had desperately wanted to talk to Judy.

'Look, try not to worry about this, Alison,' she went on. 'Judy is just . . . Well, she has a lot to think about at the moment, but everything will be fine very soon.'

'What sort of things does she have to think about?'

'Oh, to do with her work — that sort of thing.'

'But . . . ' Alison began.

'You really should have eaten your supper, dear,' Mrs Millar said brightly — too brightly.

'I'm not hungry.'

'You've been looking a lot fitter recently, Alison. Come now, love, we don't want you falling ill again. I'll just make tea for all three of us, and you can have a wee bite to eat before bedtime. You won't be able to sleep on an empty stomach.'

Alison did her best to enjoy the delicious sandwiches, but she had no appetite whatsoever. The Millars, too, were very quiet, and after a while the girl excused herself and went upstairs to bed.

That night she was glad to crawl between her soft sheets, though her mind was too disturbed for sleep. Was she really welcome in this house which she had always considered her second home? Was that the reason for Judy's attitude towards her?

Alison began to wonder if Judy resented her presence here at Calderlea . . . But no — that was absurd — Judy would never even think of such a thing.

At least, the old Judy wouldn't. But suppose Judy had changed? She had been living away from home for some time, and might have developed a completely different outlook on life.

She might even have met someone,

another man, perhaps, who was influencing her. And she *had* broken her engagement . . .

Alison eventually drifted off into a restless sleep, but she woke up heavy-eyed, unrefreshed, and with a throbbing headache. Dashing cold water on her face helped a little, and by the time she went downstairs into the kitchen, she felt much better.

She had also done a great deal of thinking, and had decided it was time she got on with her own life.

The pain of losing Alec wasn't going to go away. Wherever she went, she took it with her, and she must go back to the flat sometime, and start to work again.

She put this forward to Mr and Mrs Millar at breakfast-time, and there was no doubt about their genuine concern for her.

If Judy resented Alison acting like a daughter of the house, at least her parents did not.

'Oh, it's too soon, Alison,' Mrs Millar protested. 'Why not stay here just one

42

more week, and give yourself time to prepare?'

'I don't think I'll ever be more prepared,' Alison said. 'And I'll really have to get back to work.'

'Won't you be doing more harm than good if you start work too soon?' Mr Millar asked.

Alison smiled, then shrugged. 'Well, I'll have to ease myself in gently no matter when I start,' she said. 'I'll just have to chuck out my initial efforts until it all starts to flow smoothly again.'

'Well, if you're sure,' Mrs Millar said. 'I'll come with you.'

'No, I'll go,' Mr Millar interposed. 'I can help Alison to get the flat warmed up. And in any case — you've forgotten that Judy will be phoning tonight.'

There was silence between them, and Alison could see the constraint settling on the Millars. At least Mrs Millar will be able to talk freely with Judy, if I'm not around, Alison thought, a trifle bitterly.

Yet, in an odd sort of way, it was an

added spur to her to get on with making a new life for herself.

'I'll just go and pack my odds and ends,' she said brightly. But she had to force back the tears again when Mrs Millar took her hands in hers.

'Promise me you'll come back if you feel you need us again, Alison,' she urged. 'You must know that Walter and I are only too happy to have you here.'

'I know,' Alison whispered. 'You — you've both been wonderful to me. But I must learn to stand on my own two feet sometime, and I'm sure I'll be all right now.'

She rose with new determination and went to gather her possessions together.

★ ★ ★

Had the flat always been this dull and dreary, Alison wondered. Somehow there had never been any money to buy pretty things to brighten it up.

She thought about the small nest-egg she had put away, and she hated herself for doing it. It was almost as though she had bought Alec's death with that money. But then she pulled herself together — that was nonsense!

It was just her depression that made her think that way. She would use some of the money to change the furnishings which Alec had found perfectly adequate, but which she herself had only just managed to tolerate.

Alison sat down to a solitary tea in the small kitchen. At least Ian Thomson had been pleased to see her when she had called in for the key.

She had insisted on coming home from Calderlea on her own, as part of her new independence, and had just telephoned to assure the Millars of her safe arrival.

The long evening stretched before her, however, and she contented herself with sorting out her mail and in making plans for starting the new commission she had just received from her publishers.

She had been asked for a series of

drawings in pen and ink, her least favourite type of commission, but she was just thankful to have any kind of work to do. She wouldn't make a start till morning, when the light was good again.

The doorbell rang, jolting her out of her thoughts, and she was delighted to see Ian on the doorstep, looking very smart in a new dark suit, pale blue shirt and matching tie.

'I wondered if you'd like to come out and have dinner with me, Alison?' he invited. 'I thought it wouldn't be much fun for cooking for yourself on your first evening back.'

'Oh, Ian, what a lifesaver you are!' she said with relief. Then, seeing the happiness in Ian's eyes, she wondered if she had sounded too warm, too enthusiastic.

'You see, I — I haven't had time to do very much shopping yet,' she continued, trying to sound more matter of fact. 'I'll welcome a meal out. I'll just change out of these casual clothes.'

'They look smart enough to me,' Ian said gallantly.

'But they're hardly suitable for going out to dinner!'

She chose her new dress with the creamy lace top, thinking that she'd had little opportunity to wear it during the past few months.

Sometimes, however, she and Alec had decided on an evening out, and there had been very precious memories. I miss him very much, Alison thought, as she sat by the mirror putting the finishing touches to her make-up. It seemed unreal and incredible even now that she should be dressing up to go out with someone else.

Again she had to force back the tears and smile brightly at Ian as she walked into the living-room, hardly noticing the admiration in his eyes.

'Where to? Or do you want me to decide?' he asked.

'You decide.' She smiled, then added. 'I'll go anywhere except the Pickwick.'

'Why, did you go there with Alec?'

Ian asked. As soon as the words were out, he regretted them. Perhaps he shouldn't have spoken so naturally about Alec.

But Alison preferred it that way. 'Yes. I — I'm not quite ready yet . . . '

'Sure — I understand,' Ian said gently. 'It will take time, Alison. Anyway, I know a new place we could go to. It's only been open a few months, so we'll have to take a chance on the food. It looks nice, though.'

'Well, nothing ventured, nothing gained. Let's go!' Alison smiled.

It had been a surprisingly happy evening, she thought later, as she lay in her big double bed. Now, however, she found she was cold despite the electric blanket and the warm heaters in the room.

Tomorrow she would get a single bed, and change the furniture round here and there. That might make her feel better.

★ ★ ★

Time after time Alison had to throw her artwork into the waste-paper basket the following morning! Nothing seemed to come right. She had to concentrate really hard before she was satisfied that the basic drawing was good. Then she threw down her pen and climbed stiffly from her chair when the doorbell rang in the afternoon.

Ken Doig stood smiling to her on the landing.

'I've just been to Ian Thomson's,' he said, 'and he mentioned that you were back home.'

'Come in, Ken.' She returned his smile. 'I could do with a break for coffee, and you're invited. I'm struggling a bit with my work, I'm afraid.'

'So I see!' he said, looking at her overflowing basket.

As Alison went into the kitchen, he picked up the sketches on her drawing-board, a slight frown on his face as he studied them carefully.

He'd always admired Alison's work, but he could see that these drawings fell well short of her usual standard. No doubt they would be the next ones for the basket!

'It's taken me all day to turn out those two,' Alison said, coming into the room. 'And I have four more to do. I couldn't get them right at all.'

'And you are happy with these ones?'

'Yes. Why? Don't they look OK?'

'Oh, I — I was just thinking I'd better be careful with them,' Ken replied hastily. No doubt she was a much better judge than he. 'Eh, no sugar, Alison,' he said, changing the subject in rather a clumsy manner.

'Surely you're not slimming, Ken!'

He laughed.

'I've actually called to see if you'd like to look at the new extension. Oh, I know it will be painful for you, Alison. I know that anything to do with Alec is going to hurt you for some time, but life must go on, love.'

'It — it does hurt, Ken,' she agreed, and he reached over and gripped her fingers tightly.

'I think you should come out and see the extension now, Alison. You'll feel better afterwards, and you'll be able to accept it all that much more easily.'

She sighed. 'Well, I don't know, Ken. I've just started work again.'

'You'll do it all the better if you work yourself in gradually. You're inclined to rush headlong into things.'

'All right, then. I'll get my coat.'

★   ★   ★

Ken kept up his cheerful conversation even though Alison grew more and more quiet as they drove towards Ken's shop, where she saw that the new extension was shaping up well.

'I think the architect did a good job, don't you?' he asked her, as they gazed up at the new facade. 'He's managed to design me a modern building which is in keeping with its surroundings.'

'It's terrific, Ken,' Alison said. 'You must be very proud of it.'

Alec would have been proud of it,

too, Alison thought painfully. This time Alec's judgment hadn't been at fault. She had withheld her support without even looking to see what was involved. And now it was too late!

The words seemed to echo in her head as she walked round with Ken.

Noticing her white face, he quietly guided her towards his office, where he asked a pretty young girl to bring them coffee.

'Alec would have been happy here,' Alison said sadly. 'He really might have worked hard this time.'

'Pehaps he would,' Ken said, his voice gentle. He poured a cup of strong, hot tea. 'Here, this will perk you up. I'll come for you another day, though, Alison, and bring you back here until you get used to the place. There's no point in avoiding people or places that bring the memories back, is there?'

Illogically she thought about Judy. Was Judy avoiding her because she was afraid of her grief? Perhaps that was the reason for all this silence. Perhaps Judy didn't know how to express the sympathy she must feel.

'I won't,' she told Ken. 'I'm determined to face up to everything. All the same, I'm going to do up the flat and change round the furniture to give it a new look.'

'Now, I can help you there,' Ken said. 'Ian and I are big, strong lads. At least I am — I'm not sure about him!'

'It's a good job I don't have a piano which needs to be removed,' she told him. 'In fact, I could probably manage most of the work in the flat myself.'

'No fear!' Ken said. 'Don't you dare lay a finger on anything! Just draw a plan of where it all has to go, and we'll do it for you when we're both free.'

'Done!' Alison said, feeling warmed. She could never grumble about not having friends to turn to, even if Judy wasn't among them at the moment. And she wouldn't judge Judy until she had seen her again, and talked to her. She longed to hear from her.

A week or two later Alison received a

bitter-sweet letter from her publishers. It accompanied an all-too-familiar package — the return of her pen and ink drawings.

The accompanying letter suggested that the project was, perhaps, not quite suited to her talents, but they had another in mind. Would it be possible for her to come to London to discuss this?

Alison looked again at the work which had been returned. The publishers were absolutely right. It was poor stuff, done without heart. She could see that her lack of concentration showed up all too clearly.

Yet there was hope for her in this new project her publishers mentioned, and she was eager to take up the chance of spending a couple of nights in London. That would give her a perfect opportunity to find out more about Judy.

She had been asked to ring to make an appointment, and was slightly taken aback to be given one for the following day. She was about to tear her rejected work to pieces when she paused, then decided to put it away in her cupboard.

She had better leave the key with Ian, however, and explain about Ken's offer to move her furniture. She had worked out a new plan for rearranging it, and had ordered a new single bed.

She would also sew new curtains and cushion covers, and might even make a woollen rug in bright colours. It should all look a lot more cosy when it was finished.

Ian's eyes lit up when Alison called round to see him, but he looked taken aback when she gave him the plan for her furniture switch-round, then laughingly explained Ken's idea about the two men moving it for her.

'And this was Ken Doig's idea?'

Alison blinked, withdrawing a little. Was she, perhaps, taking Ian too much for granted? Perhaps it was an impertinence expecting him to help her like this, but she had been so sure he wouldn't mind.

'Oh, there's no need for you to help,

if you don't want to, Ian,' she said quietly. 'Ken was just throwing out ideas.'

Ian fought down his rising jealousy of Ken Doig. Trust him to see some way of giving Alison practical help!

'Of course I'll be helping,' he cried. 'Just try to stop me! We'll have this stuff shifted in no time. So you're going to London, Alison?'

'Yes.' She nodded. 'My publishers are suggesting a new project, which is really nice of them. I actually deserved the sack after the last bit of work I did for them. It was awful!' She looked crestfallen.

'I expect they know it's only a temporary set-back,' he said comfortingly.

'Anyway, you go and enjoy your visit. Try to relax and take in a few interesting sights before you come back.'

'Like what?'

'Well, the art galleries for inspiration, of course. The Victoria and Albert, maybe — and the zoo.'

'The zoo!'

'Why not? You could sit and draw the animals.'

She laughed. Ian was becoming very good at cheering her up.

★   ★   ★

Alison enjoyed the journey to London by rail, though she decided to take a taxi to the address of her publishers. It would be quicker than trying to work it out by using the Underground.

The offices weren't quite as opulent as she had imagined and that was rather comforting. So, too, was Mr Whyte, the kindly middle-aged man who interviewed her in a quiet room, the walls of which were lined with showcases full of books.

'I understand you've recently lost your husband, Mrs Drummond?' he asked.

'Yes. He — he was killed in a car accident,' she said quietly.

'How sad. You have our deepest sympathy. I'm only sorry we had to return the pen and ink drawings.'

'They were awful! I know that. I only really saw them after they came back.'

Mr Whyte smiled. 'We'll forget about them, shall we? I must say I've always liked your style. And now we're hoping to publish a new animal book for children . . . '

He went into details and as Alison listened she began to see quite clearly how the illustrations could be done.

She also forgot to be shy, and soon she was sketching furiously, offering her own suggestions and feeling more alive than she had done for months.

'Well, you've obviously cottoned on to the idea, Mrs Drummond,' Mr Whyte told her. 'Suppose you send down one or two specimen drawings, and we can OK them.'

His manner became more business-like.

'I don't have to tell you that this is a big project — the biggest we've ever offered you. It will mean a great deal of work.'

'I'll love doing it,' Alison said simply. 'It's a delightful book.'

She was surprised when she saw how long she had spent in the publisher's office. Feeling hungry, she made her way to a small hotel where she booked in and had a light meal.

When she'd finished, she decided to go to the research laboratory in the Wimbledon area, where Judy worked, and try to see her.

She had already rung the flat again, but there was still no reply.

She thought it would be best to take the Underground to Wimbledon and get a taxi from the station.

The research laboratory was a well-constructed, red-brick building enhanced with beautifully-laid-out flowerbeds. It was a busy place, with people constantly coming and going, and the staff car park was filled to capacity.

The taxi had deposited Alison at the main gates, and now she walked up towards an imposing entrance, looking about her with curiosity. How odd that this place must seem like a second home to Judy when it was so completely strange to her.

Inside the main building, Alison saw a door marked 'Enquiries,' and went forward to ring the bell. Two bright-faced, young girls were chattering happily, one of them going to answer the telephone while the other looked up from her typewriter.

'Yes?' she asked, coming over to Alison. 'Can I help you?'

'I'd like to speak to Dr Millar,' Alison said, 'Dr Judy Millar.'

'Oh, she isn't here at the moment,' the young receptionist told her. 'Just a moment, please.' She turned to her colleague who had just put down the telephone. 'Wasn't there some instruction about calls for Dr Millar?'

'Yes, they've all been referred to the head of her department — Dr Rutherford.'

'Oh yes, that's it.' The girl came back

to the window. 'Dr Rutherford is dealing with Dr Millar's calls,' she said, 'and I'm afraid he isn't in this week. He's having seven days' leave and he's taking all calls at home.'

Alison's heart sank. Only now did she realise how disappointed she was not to see her friend's happy face.

Judy was tall and elegant with beautiful brown hair and grey eyes, but her smile always made her look like a teenager again.

'Could I possibly have Dr Rutherford's address?' she asked. 'It's really very important.'

The girl weighed the situation up for a few minutes.

'OK,' she agreed at last. She went to look up a file, writing down the address. 'It isn't far from here.' She smiled as she handed over the paper. 'You could phone from the callbox in the lobby if you like.'

'No thanks, I'd rather call in person,' Alison said, her determination growing. She would not leave London until she had found Judy, and had spoken to her face to face!

'You could walk there, if you like,' the girl said helpfully, giving her directions.

'Thanks for everything,' Alison said, and set off at a brisk pace.

Soon the tall, solid houses gave way to detached residences set in gardens filled with leafy trees and well-tended flowerbeds, each one separated from the neighbouring house by high walls.

Alison found the address she was looking for, and her steps faltered a little as she walked up to the beautifully-designed residence and rang the bell.

The sun was still shining, throwing shadows on to the lawn, and as she rang yet again, she could hear the click of a side gate and hurried footsteps coming round the corner from the direction of the gardens at the back of the house.

A tall girl with shining smooth brown hair stood staring at her, shielding her eyes from the sun.

'Yes?' she asked. 'Can I help you?'

Then — 'Alison! You! What on earth are you doing here?'

Alison's eyes widened and her face went white with shock. The voice and gestures were Judy's but at first glance the tall, slender girl bore absolutely no facial resemblance to Judy Millar!

A Lifeline

Suddenly, the girl turned on her heel and disappeared round the back of the house. Alison was about to follow but it was too late, the girl had gone.

For a long moment Alison stood on the doorstep of Dr Rutherford's house hardly knowing what to do.

A few moments before she'd been face to face with Judy, or so she'd thought. And though she'd obviously recognised Alison, Alison hadn't recognised her! Yet it must have been Judy — the girl had had all Judy's mannerisms!

Alison was bewildered but now she was here she was determined to find out what was going on.

With renewed determination she rang the doorbell again, deciding she wasn't going to leave until she had got to the bottom of the matter. Somehow she must have some answers.

She kept her finger on the bell, then she tried the door, but it was locked against her.

Alison bit her lip, wondering if she should try the back entrance, when she heard the sound of footsteps coming down the drive. A moment later a smartly-dressed elderly lady walked up to her, looking at her with interest.

'Can I help you?' she asked. 'I'm Mrs Rutherford.'

Alison's cheeks grew pink but she nodded with relief.

'Oh, hello,' she said. 'I've called to see Dr Rutherford.'

'Well, he's out, I'm afraid, but he should be home soon. Would you like to leave a message, or would you prefer to wait?'

Mrs Rutherford had stepped forward and was opening the door with her key.

'I'm Alison Drummond,' Alison told her. 'I've actually called to enquire about my friend, Dr Judy Millar . . . '

She saw the sudden stillness in the

older woman and for a long moment Mrs Rutherford hesitated before pushing open the door.

'Please come in,' she said quietly, and Alison followed her into a large square hall, which was decorated in cool shades of green and white.

Mrs Rutherford led the way into a spacious drawing-room filled with comfortable chintz-covered chairs and well-polished furniture. Curtains were drawn over the windows, and a coal fire cast flickering shadows on the walls. Mrs Rutherford invited Alison to sit down, pulling up a chair towards the open fire.

'The sunshine has been lovely,' she said pleasantly, 'but it gets chilly at this time of day. You — you've come to ask about Dr Millar?'

'Yes, I'd like to see her,' Alison said firmly. 'I know she's here, and I'd like a word with her.'

Mrs Rutherford bit her lip and turned to poke up the fire.

'I'm afraid I'll have to ask you to wait

and talk to my son,' she said uneasily. 'He's dealing with Dr Millar's affairs.'

Alison looked at the older woman's discomfort and her bewilderment grew.

'Mrs Rutherford, I've known Judy Millar all my life,' she said clearly, 'and I love her like a sister. I know there's something very wrong. Won't you please tell me what it is?'

'I think it's time I told you myself.'

Alison whirled round with a startled exclamation when she heard Judy's voice behind her, and Mrs Rutherford stood up with obvious relief.

'I'll go and make some tea, Judy dear,' she said, 'It will give you two young ladies a chance to talk.'

Alison scarcely heard her. She was gazing at the figure that had come into the room and now stood in the shadows by a door in the far wall.

'Judy?' Alison whispered. 'Is it you?'

She stepped forward to see more clearly the face that was obscured in shadow.

Judy spoke sharply. 'No! Don't come

any closer, Alison.'

'It *is* you, Judy!' Alison stopped in mid-stride. 'What — what's wrong? What's happened?'

She still couldn't see her friend's face clearly, but she could see that the hairstyle was completely changed. Gone was the short, cropped style that Judy had always worn.

'I've been in an accident,' Judy said, rather harshly. 'At the lab. I just don't want you to see me. It's my face. You shouldn't have come here, Alison.'

'I didn't know,' Alison replied softly.

'No, of course you didn't! Oh, what's the use! I can't very well hide for ever.'

With that she stepped forward out of the shadows towards Alison. It was Judy — but yet not Judy — who stood before her. The long straight brown hair framing and partly obscuring her face made a difference. The grey eyes regarding Alison were the same, but there was a kind of anguish in them now, not the humorous sparkle that Alison remembered.

But Judy's features had altered and at first sight in the shaded room she looked quite different.

'Go on, have a good look,' she said, her voice still harsh. She put a hand to her face and brushed back the fringe from her forehead and suddenly Alison realised what had happened. The thin scar left by a skilled surgeon showed clearly.

Next, her friend held back the wing of hair that fell across her cheek. Again the thin but vivid scar in front of Judy's ear stood out. She let her hair fall back into place and the subtly-changed face that the plastic surgery had given her looked back at Alison.

Abruptly Judy turned away and sat down in the chair so recently occupied by Mrs Rutherford.

'Oh, Judy, I'm so sorry,' Alison said. She felt so inadequate. She wanted to say much, much more to comfort her friend — her best friend. She swallowed hard. She didn't want Judy to see the tears that welled up in her eyes.

'Do you want to tell me about it?' she said quietly. 'Sometimes talking helps . . . '

'Can't you see? You've got eyes in your head, Alison. You can see the — the mess my face is in.'

Almost instinctively, her hand again went up to shield her face from Alison's searching eyes, and she turned away.

Judy sighed wearily.

'It was an accident at the lab, that's all. I just happened to be in the wrong place at the wrong time.'

'Oh, Judy!' Alison said, her voice full of sympathy. 'Why didn't you tell me?'

'Well, I look awful now, but I looked really hideous then. I — I didn't want anyone to know until I'd had plastic surgery. But they've done their best for me and . . . ' Judy's voice cracked, and then she turned away again with her hands over her face.

'It's been like an awful nightmare, Alison. I — I can't get used to the fact that it's happened to me. Can't you understand why I didn't want to see anyone?'

* * *

Gradually Alison was beginning to understand a little, but deep down she felt oddly hurt that Judy hadn't confided in her. She had never believed there was anything in the world they couldn't have told one another.

And yet weren't there some things she hadn't told Judy? She remembered some of the small, unhappy incidents in her married life which had hurt her deeply, yet had meant little to Alec.

She had buried them deep within herself, a queer sense of pride forbidding her to confide in anyone else — even Judy.

'Oh, Judy, I'm sorry,' she said quietly. 'I do understand.'

Her warm love and sympathy for her best friend became uppermost in her heart and she reached out to take

Judy's hand. For a moment she felt that Judy was responding, then Alison could feel her pulling away.

'That's OK, Alison. I'll get used to it. They — they all tell me how lucky I was that my eyes weren't affected. I'll just have to keep reminding myself to count my blessings, won't I?'

Judy tried to laugh lightly, but it sounded hollow even to herself.

'I'll just have to forget how awful I look.'

'You don't look awful!' Alison cried. 'Honestly, Judy. The scars will disappear completely in time. It's marvellous what . . . '

But Judy's hand went up to her face again.

'No! I don't want to talk about it! That's enough about me. What about you? I was so sorry when I heard about Alec. How are you coping?'

Alison tried to wrench her thoughts away from Judy. She had forgotten about her own troubles, and it seemed as though her whole being had been concentrated on Judy. Now she had to gather herself together.

'Oh, I'm coping,' she said huskily. 'I'm trying to change the flat a little, though.'

'Here's Mrs Rutherford with the tea,' Judy said, and got up to help the older woman with the tray. 'I forgot to introduce you properly.'

She smiled at her hostess.

'Mrs Rutherford had kindly allowed me to stay here for a short while since I left hospital. Dr Rutherford is my chief . . . '

'Who's taking my name in vain?'

Alison swung round as a tall, thin man with dark hair, greying at the temples, walked in.

'Oh, there you are, Charles,' Mrs Rutherford said, smiling. 'He can always hear the clink of teacups, Mrs Drummond. This is my son and, Charles, this is Judy's friend, Mrs Alison Drummond.'

Alison found that Dr Rutherford had a firm handshake and his dark blue eyes were very keen as he looked at her closely.

'I came along to ask about Judy,' she explained. 'I — I was rather anxious.'

'Very natural,' he agreed. He picked up a plate of biscuits, offering them to both girls.

Judy shook her head. 'I don't feel very hungry.'

Mrs Rutherford turned to look at her closely, hearing the fatigue in the girl's voice.

'Oh, my dear, I do think you ought to go back up to bed,' she said with concern. 'We have to be careful of Judy's health for a little while yet,' she explained to Alison. 'I think, if you'll excuse us, I ought to take her upstairs.'

'It's time I went in any case,' Alison said, glancing at her watch.

'No, finish your tea. Don't rush away,' Mrs Rutherford said.

'We must finish off the pot between us, anyway,' Dr Rutherford said, pouring her a second cup. 'Waste not, want not.'

Alison turned to Judy, then bent forward and kissed her cheek. Judy looked too tired to care.

'I'll be in touch,' Alison said.

'OK,' Judy replied. 'I'll — I'll see you then, some other time.'

'I'm afraid I really will have to go,' Alison said when she was left alone with Dr Rutherford. 'I was just so worried and, well, rather puzzled over what could have happened to Judy.'

'I know,' Dr Rutherford said gently. 'What are your plans? Are you staying in London overnight?'

'Yes. In fact, I'm staying for two nights,' Alison said. 'I've booked in at the Greenbank Hotel, and I thought I'd like to do some shopping tomorrow.'

'Could you spare the time to have dinner with me tomorrow evening?' Dr Rutherford asked. 'I could come to your hotel, if that would be easier. Would that be possible?'

His expression was serious.

'I feel there's a great deal we could discuss. As you see, Judy is still far from well and I feel you might be able to help.'

'Very well, Dr Rutherford,' Alison said as she rose to go.

It was her turn to look at him speculatively. He wasn't as old as she'd first thought, and was probably still in his mid-thirties. On her way back to the hotel, Alison's thoughts were on Dr Rutherford as well as Judy.

Could it be there was more to their relationship than simply being professional colleagues? Alison had understood very easily why Judy had broken her engagement to Blair. In the initial shock of her disfigurement, it would be the most natural thing for her to do. But now she wondered if that broken engagement hadn't secretly pleased Dr Rutherford.

Alison shook off her thoughts as she left the Underground station to walk to her hotel. Maybe she was imagining things. Perhaps she just wanted something to exist which would convince Judy that she was still very attractive to other people.

Judy hated her new face, and was going to need a lot of persuading that other people didn't hate it as well. Yet if Alison was honest with herself, it was the old Judy whom she longed to see, and that night, in her lonely hotel room, Alison wept into her pillow.

Somehow she seemed to have lost that old Judy, and it might take some time to get her back.

★   ★   ★

London always cheered Alison up. There was so much to do and so much to see. She had resolved to treat herself to a new suit for the winter which would soon be upon them, and she spent a few hours wandering round the shops, deliberately looking at new styles and colours before deciding on a blue wool.

After a small inward argument about extravagance, she also chose a pretty dress to wear that evening. It wouldn't help Judy if she worried herself sick over her.

Remembering her dinner engagement, she had a light lunch in a small coffee bar, then wandered round one or two art galleries and museums.

She was weary and footsore by the time she returned to her hotel, but a warm bath soon put fresh energy into her, and the new dress looked quite suitable for her dinner date.

She knew, however, that clothes wouldn't be important as far as Dr Rutherford was concerned. Their main concern would be Judy.

When he walked into the hotel lounge, he looked very smart in his dark suit and sparkling white shirt. Alec had always preferred casual clothes for practically every occasion, but Alison liked more formal clothes.

'Well,' Dr Rutherford asked, as they were shown to their table, 'did you have a good day? Judy tells me you're a famous artist, so I expect the oil sheiks would have to settle for second place when you went shopping today!'

Alison laughed, her eyes crinkling merrily.

'I'm not at all famous and my spending power is very limited,' she said. 'The oil sheiks are quite safe.'

'But I thought you had come to see your publisher. That sounds pretty high powered.'

'Maybe, but I only came to see them after a terrible failure on my part. Fortunately, I've been given a second chance. I only hope I'll be able to produce the goods this time.'

'Sometimes it's wonderful to have a second chance,' Dr Rutherford said. 'It can be great to be able to start all over again.'

Their eyes met and Alison knew he was thinking about Judy, but again she wondered if he was alluding to Judy's new face, or to the relationship between them.

'Are you and Judy close colleagues

at the research laboratory, Dr Rutherford?' she asked.

'Yes, we've worked together ever since she came to Wimbledon,' he said, signalling the waiter. 'We've worked on a great many projects.'

He ordered the meal and turned to her again.

'What did Judy tell you about the accident?'

'Only that it happened,' Alison said. 'She probably didn't think I'd understand.'

'Then she didn't say that she took the full brunt of the explosion after pushing a young laboratory technician out of the way?'

His expression became very grave.

'Susan Reynolds is young and very inexperienced. She was probably nervous and Judy saw what was going to happen when Sue made the very mistake she had warned her about. They were both injured, but Sue's burns weren't serious. Her right shoulder was the only part affected.'

Dr Rutherford sighed, obviously distressed that his staff had been injured.

'She's out of hospital and perfectly fit again, but Judy took it on the face, and only her eyes were protected. It — it made a mess of her. The plastic surgery which has been done is . . . Well, quite frankly it's a miracle. You just don't know what marvels they've performed for her.'

Alison nodded slowly. Judy looked different, that was true, but the scars would fade in time.

'Judy's real scars are inside,' Dr Rutherford said. 'That's why I wanted to speak to you.' He paused, smiling. 'Eat up, though. How's your steak?'

'Delicious.' Alison smiled back, though she had little appetite for her meal.

'A night out will do you good, Mrs Drummond. I'm quite sure of that.'

'Please just call me Alison,' she said. 'It's easier.'

He smiled and nodded.

'I was sorry to hear about your tragic loss,' he said quietly. 'Your husband must have been very young.'

★ ★ ★

She turned away a little to hide the sudden rush of tears. Genuine sympathy always had the power to open the wound.

'Yes. I went to stay with Judy's parents. Their home is a place of refuge for me, just as yours is for Judy. All my life I've thought of Mr and Mrs Millar almost as though they were my foster parents. I — I love them both.'

He stared at her keenly. 'Then can you think of any reason why Judy should avoid going home to Calderlea?'

Alison shook her head.

'Not unless she doesn't want to see Blair — Blair Walker, her fiancé. Well, he used to be engaged to . . . '

'Yes, I know all about that,' Dr Rutherford said quietly. 'But this problem has more to do with actually going home. She seems to shrink from it — from her mother, in particular. I just wondered what sort of woman she is.'

'She's a wonderful woman!' Alison cried. 'She's the most wonderful woman I know, and she loves Judy very much. So does Mr Millar. Judy's the light of their lives.'

'Yet she hesitates to go to them, even now when she's so much better, and almost able to travel home. The hospital authorities would still like her to rest for perhaps another week, but after that it's just a matter of a good rest, good food and fresh air.'

His smile was wry. 'From what you say, the ideal place for that is Calderlea.'

'Oh, yes, it is,' Alison said. 'It put me back on my feet.'

Yet her expression was growing more thoughtful. She was remembering, again, the strange look of reserve on Mrs Millar's face, and her refusal to discuss Judy.

Alison had thought it was Judy who resented her presence at Calderlea, but now she wasn't so sure. She felt there was something she still didn't understand.

'Still, Judy agrees that she'll have to go home sometime,' Dr Rutherford continued. 'The thing is, I was wondering if they'd think it was an impertinence on my part if I offered to travel with Judy, and perhaps stay at Calderlea for a short while to see her settled in.

'There must surely be a hotel nearby?' he went on. 'I can extend my leave. I just feel she needs all the support she can get at this time.'

Alison looked at him and for the first time there was a hint of uncertainty in his eyes.

'I'm sure they'd give you a very warm welcome,' she said quietly. 'They'd be so grateful for the way you're trying to help Judy. Mind you, I think they'd prefer you to stay at Hillside. It's quite a big house.'

He nodded and began to toy with his cheese and biscuits.

'Well, I still feel I'd be walking into a situation I don't really understand,' he said slowly. 'I think you could help, Alison, even if you can spare only a few days of your time. Couldn't you come up to Calderlea at the same time?'

He obviously wanted her to very much.

'Perhaps Judy just needs the initial push back into the family fold again. Maybe I've got it all wrong, but I feel that with two of us there, helping Judy — and her parents may need help, too — then perhaps everything can be sorted out.'

Alison looked at him thoughtfully. For a brief moment she was remembering the demanding new comission she was about to start, but she didn't hesitate.

'If you really think I'd be able to help, then of course I'll come. I owe the Millars so much already. But how does Judy feel about all this?'

He grinned.

'She doesn't know about it yet, but I'm sure your visit has broken the ice. I think she'll cling to you like a lifeline. She'll have to face the local people again sometime, and who better to help her do it than yourself?

'Please don't say anything to Judy's parents, though, until Judy agrees,' he went on. 'I'll telephone them and see how they feel about the idea.'

Alison nodded.

They had coffee in the lounge, then Dr Rutherford looked at his watch.

'Time to go, I'm afraid. Well, I've enjoyed our evening, Mrs Drummond — I mean Alison — even if we did have some very serious matters to discuss.'

Alison smiled, thinking that she had enjoyed it, too.

'I'll get in touch as soon as I arrive in Edinburgh with Judy,' he promised.

'I'll look forward to that,' Alison assured him, and watched his tall figure striding out of the hotel. Judy was very lucky to have a friend like Charles Rutherford, she thought. If anyone could bring some joy back into her life, then surely he could.

★ ★ ★

Alison travelled home next day, but with every passing mile her thoughts were becoming more and more jumbled. Judy had never been vain about her appearance, and although she looked slightly different now, she was still very attractive.

Surely, after Judy had got over the shock of the accident, she would be her old self again?

If she was going to help Judy at all, as Charles Rutherford had asked, then she would have to concentrate on trying to bring out Judy's former personality again. That wouldn't be an easy task, especially if she was reluctant to go home.

That was a puzzle. Alison would have expected her to rush home straightaway. She'd thought it out from every angle, but Calderlea still seemed the most logical refuge for her friend.

When she reached Edinburgh, Alison was feeling tired and rather depressed, so that Ian Thomson's smile of welcome wavered a little when he saw her white face.

'You look as though you've overdone the sightseeing in London, Alison,' he chided her. 'You're worn out.'

'Oh, I didn't do very much sightseeing, Ian,' she told him. 'Could I have my key please?'

He handed it to her, his eyes alight with anticipation.

'I'll go back to the flat with you,' he offered. 'Ken Doig and I managed to rearrange all your furniture for you. Your new bed has arrived, by the way, and we put that up, too. We moved the old one into the spare bedroom until you decide what you want to do with it.'

Alison would have preferred to go home on her own because she longed to relax in a warm bath, and to make herself a good cup of tea, just as she liked it. Still, she was grateful to Ian for all his work on her behalf.

The flat looked quite strange when she walked into it, and for a long moment Alison was filled with deep regret that she had ever decided to change things. Her whole world seemed to be changing about her and familiar things were becoming important to her sense of security.

Now the flat didn't look like home to her at all. Some of her old furniture had been inclined to appear heavy, but the new layout had diminished that, so that the flat seemed remarkably bright and airy.

It was a great improvement, but it still looked strange and unreal, and she would have to get to know it all over again — just as she would with Judy, she thought sadly.

Ian was eagerly showing her everything he and Ken had done on her behalf.

'Now wait till you see the bedroom,' he said happily, opening the door. 'Is this how you pictured it, Alison? I think it looks great.'

It's a lovely bedroom, but it belongs to someone else, Alison thought. Nothing in it seemed to belong to her. She stared at the strange new bed, with the patterned covers she had chosen and ordered.

Her dressing-table looked different, set at that angle, and her wardrobe seemed to have grown smaller now that it was standing it its new place in an alcove.

Again the room looked a great deal bigger and more airy, and there was a new chair which was a perfect match for the bed.

I didn't order that! Alison thought. She remembered admiring the chair in the shop, but she had decided against it, feeling she had spent enough. Now it had been delivered with the other things by mistake.

'I really must thank you and Ken,'

she told Ian rather lamely. It wasn't their fault that she found the changes so unsettling. 'It was very good of you both to go to so much trouble. This chair will have to go back, though.'

'Oh, no!' Ian said quickly. 'That's OK. It's yours. I knew you liked it, so I — I bought it for you.'

Alison flushed pink. It was one thing to accept a little help in rearranging her furniture, but it was quite another to accept the furniture itself!

'Well, I'm sorry but I'll have to ask you to take it back, Ian,' she said very quietly. 'I can't accept gifts like this from you. As I say, I — I'm very grateful for your help, but I prefer to buy my own furniture, thank you.'

Ian's face had gone white. 'But surely — it's only a chair after all!'

'A very expensive one, Ian. I know. I saw it when I bought the bed. I'm sorry, but I can't accept it.'

Ian looked hurt. 'OK, Alison,' he said stiffly. 'If that's how you feel, I'll arrange to have it collected. I just thought it would be a pleasant surprise for you.'

He turned on his heel, and Alison heard the door of the flat closing quietly. She went into the kitchen and sat down on her oldest chair, feeling the tears beginning to well up.

Now she had hurt Ian, who'd only been trying to make her homecoming a happy one. But she was reluctant to accept anything from anyone at the moment.

She only wanted her independence, and she did not want anyone giving her expensive gifts. He must be made to understand that.

★   ★   ★

The following morning, Alison called in to see Ian and to apologise for her abrupt behaviour, even though she hadn't changed her mind about the chair.

After a few minutes Ian relaxed a little, but Alison knew he was still hurt.

He, in his turn, could see that his friendship with Alison wasn't as close as he'd hoped. Nevertheless he could take an interest in her new project for her publishers.

'I'll need new paints,' she said. 'The detail in the work is really important and the tints have to be as subtle as possible. It won't be easy, but I'll enjoy the challenge. I know I'll have to pull out all the stops on this project, Ian.'

'I bet you'll do a great job,' he encouraged her. 'I hope you'll let me see the paintings before you post them.'

'Of course I will,' she said. 'Still, there won't be anything to send off if I don't get down to some work.'

Over the next week Alison spent long hours at her drawing board, discarding any work which had even the faintest flaw. She forgot to look at her new surroundings, and gradually it all became familiar and acceptable to her.

Looking up one morning, as a shaft of pale winter sunlight entered the room, she decided she liked it all very much.

Yet Judy was always on her mind, and when she tried to imagine Judy as she was now, it was always the old Judy who intruded. Would she ever get used to the new one, as she was getting used to the flat?

Somehow, seeing the change-round here, and her own reaction to it, she felt she understood more clearly Judy's feelings, which must be many times more acute.

How she must have suffered, Alison thought, and how much physical pain she must have gone through. This was an aspect which hadn't really got through to her before.

As she posted her work to the publishers Alison reflected that she might be required to start the main part of the project just when Judy needed her most. But her friend would have to come first.

The following day Ken Doig called to see her, and this time Alison was able to thank him sincerely for helping to move her furniture.

'I wasn't sure that I liked it at first, Ken,' she said, smiling. 'I'm afraid I — I wasn't as grateful as I ought to have been to Ian. But I'm used to it now and I really love it.'

'Well, it looks fine to me, Alison,' Ken said, though he sounded rather distant. He began to stride up and down, a habit of his when he was nervous.

'Is there anything wrong, Ken?' she asked.

He bit his lip, then turned to face her.

'Well, yes, actually there is. But I don't want to worry you unduly.' He paused, hesitant.

Alison raised her eyebrows at him. 'Well?' she urged.

'I'm looking for some bills. Receipts, actually. I gave . . . Alec was looking after some payments for me, just before . . . They're probably in that briefcase of his. Or maybe there are some papers . . . '

His voice tailed away and a cold finger of alarm touched Alison.

'I hate to ask you to look through his things, but it is important that I find these bills. Here's a list of the firms involved.'

She took the sheet of paper he held out to her and she looked at it without really seeing it. She had managed to dispose of a great many of Alec's personal possessions, but the task had become increasingly painful to her since each one held a memory which somehow grew more precious with time.

Now she would have to go through the papers in his desk.

'I'll look for them, Ken,' she agreed. 'I'll let you know.'

'Thanks, Alison. I'd do it myself, if that would help. I hate to be the cause of more pain for you.'

She nodded, knowing he understood. But it didn't help at all.

Alison put off her search until the afternoon, feeling that she could tackle it better when all her normal duties were out of the way.

Alec's papers were in a mess, but somehow the sight of them brought him very close and she could only remember his happy-go-lucky nature which caused him to lump everything together.

Sandwiched between letters and old bills from previous enterprises, she would find small mementos of their life together.

For a long time she sat gazing at a birthday card, lovingly chosen and lovingly kept, and an amusing sketch she had done of him when they had laughed together one evening after he'd had some small success and was in a buoyant mood.

Oh, Alec, she thought, her heart sore. How empty my life is without you!

Suddenly the telephone shrilled, making her jump, and she picked it up absently.

'Hello, Alison,' Dr Rutherford's deep voice said. 'I'm at Waverly Station, and I have Judy with me. I wonder if we may come along and see you now?'

Tension At Calderlea

Alison's heart leapt when she heard Dr Rutherford's deep voice on the telephone. So he and Judy were in Edinburgh!

'I'll get a taxi,' he was saying, 'and from what Judy says, we'll be seeing you very shortly, if that's convenient.'

'Of course it's convenient,' Alison assured him. 'I'm just happy that she's back home again. How is she feeling after the journey?'

'Bearing up very well,' Dr Rutherford assured her. 'But I'll be thankful when we reach your flat. Judy tires easily at the moment.'

'I'll see you as soon as possible then,' said Alison, and replaced the receiver.

Looking round the flat, she thought it had seldom looked less tidy. It had occurred to her that the bills which Ken Doig had asked for would be in Alec's briefcase, which was standing beside the desk.

It had been returned to her with all Alec's personal possessions after the accident. So far she had not been able to bring herself to go through everything. But there was no time now.

The fire would have to be lit and the flat tidied and dusted in a very short space of time. She and Judy were well used to accepting one another's disorder, but Charles Rutherford was used to a charming, well-run home.

Alison did her best to make the flat comfortable and the bell rang as she plumped up the last cushion. Rather nervously she went to open the door.

Judy stood there quietly, a headscarf covering part of her face. Her new hairstyle was again pulled forward over her forehead.

'Hello, Alison,' she said quietly.

'Oh, Judy, it's wonderful to have you back again,' said Alison huskily, then she turned to smile at Dr Rutherford.

'I think we're both thankful to be

here,' he told her, smiling, as he carried in the luggage which the taxi driver had dumped on the landing.

'Alison, did you know that it's impossible to get a really refreshing cup of tea on a train journey?' he added.

She was laughing. 'I hadn't forgotten,' she said. 'The kettle's boiling and I've warmed the pot.'

'You've just earned my undying gratitude,' he told her, and she laughed again, then turned to look at Judy more soberly.

Judy had removed her coat and scarf, but Alison could see the instinctive reaching up to touch her hair, making sure that it covered the scars on her forehead. It seemed that Judy would never get used to accepting her scars, and could see them only as ugly marks on what had been her beautiful complexion.

'I hope you're both ready for a meal,' said Alison brightly.

Her heart was sore for Judy, but she recognised that constant sympathy would not help her. It would be better to leave her alone for the time being.

'Not that I claim to be a good cook,' she added as she turned to Dr Rutherford. 'In fact, when I'm working at my drawing board, I tend to forget about the pans on the stove, and I must hold the record for burnt offerings!

'Alec used to . . . ' she took a deep breath ' . . . used to tease me a bit.'

'I'm not awfully hungry,' said Judy, sinking down on to the settee.

'A meal cooked by Alison will do you all the good in the world,' said Charles Rutherford, sitting beside her. 'Even if she has burned it!

'Small helpings, please. Doctor's orders,' he added, smiling at Alison.

'I'll pull up a table in front of the fire,' she suggested, 'and we can all relax with a plate and a fork.

'When are you expected at Calderlea?' she asked Judy.

Her friend shrugged, and again it was Dr Rutherford who answered the question.

'As soon as possible,' he told Alison, 'but I don't think Judy can travel any further this evening, even if it is only an hour away. If you can put her up, I think she ought to stay here tonight.'

'The spare bedroom is all ready,' said Alison, 'and I have a bed which I can make up in here . . . '

'No, there's no need for that,' said Dr Rutherford quickly. 'Surely there must be a hotel where I can get bed and breakfast?'

Alison nodded. 'There's one at the corner of the street. I can telephone for you, if you like.'

'I would be grateful,' Dr Rutherford told her. 'And who said you couldn't cook? This casserole is delicious, even Judy is eating it.'

'I know exactly what to eat if Alison cooks it,' said Judy, and there was a spark of the old mischief in her eyes. 'Eat her casseroles, but avoid her sausages. Her cheesecake isn't bad either.'

'Well, I'll have to think twice about

giving you a piece after insulting my sausages,' said Alison in mock offence, though her eyes were glowing.

It was lovely to see that some of the old Judy still sparkled inside the quiet girl who sat by the fireside.

She looked very tired, however, after she had eaten her cheesecake, and Alison helped her to bed in the spare room, then fixed up Dr Rutherford's accommodation.

'I'll see you in the morning then, about nine,' he told her. 'Or will that be too early?'

'No, I'm a lark — Alec was the owl.'

'I'm a lark, too.' He smiled. 'Sometimes, on holiday, I've even watched the sunrise.'

'Best time of the day,' Alison agreed, and again they laughed together.

Her mood sobered when she returned to the kitchen and set about washing up the supper dishes before going to bed.

Judy must have taken a sleeping pill, she thought, when she went into the spare bedroom to look down on her friend, and to leave her a carafe of iced water which Judy liked to have by her bedside.

Silently Alison crawled into her own bed, but it was a long time before she slept.

★   ★   ★

It was almost eight o'clock when Alison rose next morning, but after a quick shower she felt refreshed, and she carried enough orange juice, toast and marmalade, and coffee for two into Judy's bedroom.

At first Judy's grey eyes sparkled at her happily, then it seemed that awareness came as she gradually woke up, and sat up in bed, once again pulling at her hair.

'You're too sensitive about that,' Alison told her mildly.

Judy's face darkened. 'Would you like it to be you?' she asked harshly, and Alison had no reply.

She would not like to bear such scars, she thought, but in a way she *did* bear scars even if they were buried deep inside. They might start to heal more easily if she could talk about them, but there was no-one to talk to.

Judy had more than her fair share of her own worries without listening to hers.

'Is that enough orange juice?' she asked.

'Oh — yes — sorry that I snapped, Alison,' said Judy. 'I — I know you're doing your best. I'm beastly these days.'

'That's all right,' said Alison quickly. 'Do you want marmalade on your toast?'

'I don't think I really want any . . . Oh, all right, half a slice. I suppose I'd better get up and find some clothes. I've got to go home sometime.'

'Why don't you want to go home?' Alison asked bluntly.

'Because — because your bed is too comfortable and I feel lazy,' she said, obviously glad to have thought of an excuse. 'If I don't get up now, I shall stay here all day!'

Dr Rutherford arrived while Alison was in the midst of tidying up and he immediately began to help.

This was a new experience, thought Alison, to see a man doing housework. Alec had considered that a woman's place lay firmly in the home, and that Alison's work as an artist ought to come a poor second to his creature comforts.

Alison washed up, then rinsed through the tea-towels. The phone rang and Charles Rutherford answered it.

'For you, Alison,' he said, poking his head round the door. 'I think it's your publishers.'

Alison took the telephone, her cheeks flushed with pleasure when she heard Mr Whyte's voice praising the work she had sent and asking her to go ahead with the project.

'You'd like the final set of paintings to be ready in eight weeks?' she asked.

'I should think that would give you

plenty of time, Mrs Drummond?' said Mr Whyte, a question in his voice.

'Oh, of course, Mr Whyte,' said Alison hurriedly. 'That — that will be fine.'

Nevertheless, her eyes were thoughtful as she replaced the receiver. She would have to leave her work in order to go to Calderlea with Judy. Each day away from her drawing-board would be one day less for carrying out the intricate drawing and painting which the new project demanded.

'Is it going to make things difficult for you?'

Alison started out of her reverie as Charles Rutherford came to stand beside her.

'Oh — er . . . ' she began, but he interrupted.

'Your project. I couldn't help overhearing,' he explained. 'Is it going to present you with difficulties?'

'No, of course not,' she denied. 'I've got heaps of time. I'll do those paintings in no time.'

He nodded, accepting her explanation though his eyes were thoughtful.

'Do you need anything fixed with a screwdriver while I'm here?' he asked. 'You might as well make use of a chap while you've got him in the house.'

She laughed.

'No, it's all right, thanks very much. Ian Thomson and Ken Doig — they're both old friends — have attended to that.'

'Talk of the devil!' She had picked up the telephone again as it shrilled beside her, and this time it was Ken who was speaking.

'Did you find those bills for me, Alison?' he asked, his voice anxious.

'Not yet, Ken.'

'Suppose I come round and help?'

'Well . . . ' she hesitated, ' . . . and you want to come just now, Ken?'

Suddenly she was aware that Judy had come into the room and was gesturing frantically, so she asked Ken to hold the line, putting her hand over the mouthpiece.

'I don't want to see Ken,' Judy hissed. 'I don't want to see him just yet.'

Alison bit her lip, then nodded. 'It — it isn't convenient at the moment Ken,' she said rather lamely. She could hear his quick indrawn breath.

'Very well, Alison, but I'd like to get this cleared up.'

'I'll ring you back,' she said hastily, and put the receiver down.

Judy stared at her dumbly, then she turned away.

'I'm sorry, Alison,' she said, 'I just don't feel up to seeing anyone I know just yet. And Ken might fuss.'

★   ★   ★

'Are you two girls nearly ready?' asked Charles. 'Suppose I start to load your cases into Alison's car?' He looked meaningfully at Alison and she knew that the quicker they got Judy to Calderlea, the better.

'You go ahead,' she said. 'I've just got

some papers to find for Ken, then I must take my key to Ian. I'll try not to keep you too long.'

She had not been able to bring herself to look into Alec's briefcase before, but now it seemed easy with the urgency of the journey to Calderlea propelling her on.

Quickly, she searched through Alec's papers, and in a short while she had found the bills. But — weren't they supposed to be receipted, she wondered. Hadn't Ken said he'd given Alec the money to pay these bills?

If so . . . If so . . . why were they *bills*, and not receipts?

Frantically she began to search through all of Alec's papers, half aware that Charles and Judy were now ready to make the journey to Calderlea.

Yet she must find those receipts, thought Alison, rather desperately.

Her mouth dry, Alison began to repack the papers, knowing she would find nothing more which was relevant to those bills. She put them into an envelope, her mind busy.

She couldn't discuss them with Ken over the telephone without Charles and Judy overhearing, and if she asked them to wait while she sorted it out, they would see that she was upset.

'I'll take these round to Ian Thomson's,' she said briskly. 'I always leave my key there. I shan't be long, Judy. Oh, and I'd better tell Ken I've got them.'

She picked up the telephone and a moment later she was talking to Ken.

'I've found those bills,' she said, her voice strained and rather unnatural. 'I'm leaving them at Ian's for you, Ken. I — I'll have to see you later about them because I'm going up to Calderlea for a short while.'

'Is there anything wrong, Alison?' Ken asked quickly.

'Oh, no,' she said airily. 'Everything's fine, Ken. I'll be in touch. See you.'

★　★　★

For a long time Ken stood with the receiver still in his hand. Alison had not sounded like herself at all, and he was annoyed with himself for asking about the bills. Yet they were very important, he reminded himself, biting his lip.

But it had obviously upset Alison to go through Alec's papers so soon. In fact, it had upset her so much that she was running up to Calderlea again.

He ran a hand through his hair, wondering how he could ask Alison to go through Alec's personal things. What had he done with the money?

Surely he couldn't have spent it in such a short time! But there had been plenty of time for him to pay those bills, but he had not done so, and that wasn't making things at all easy.

Ian Thomson's eyes lit up when Alison hurried into the shop, her cheeks flushed though her eyes were dulled and rather anxious.

'Hello, Alison,' he greeted her warmly, his smile fading a little when he looked into her eyes. 'Oh dear, didn't you land that project after all?'

'Oh — the project . . . Yes, I landed it OK, Ian. I've been given the go-ahead to have it done in eight weeks' time.'

'That's wonderful! I've got those new brushes you wanted,' he told her.

'Thanks, Ian,' she said mechanically. 'I'll have to hurry, though. I've only called to leave my key and this letter for Ken. It's some papers of his which were among Alec's things. I'll see you when I get back.'

'Where from?'

'Oh, Calderlea,' she said as she made for the door. 'I don't know how long I'll be away. Cheerio, Ian, and thanks again.'

Ian looked at the envelope in his hands, and the key to Alison's flat. Surely she wasn't still upset with him for buying that bedroom chair!

But no, it was more than that, thought Ian. There was something troubling Alison deeply, and Ian weighed the envelope for Ken thought-fully in his hands. If Ken Doig had been upsetting her, he would have something to say, he decided.

Alison hurried back to the car, apologising to Judy and Dr Rutherford for keeping them waiting.

She'd had to do some last-minute shopping. Since she worked long hours at home, her life wasn't always as well organised as it might be.

'It's all right,' said Judy, laughing a little. 'I've told Charles you're always like the cow's tail!'

'Oh, Judy!'

Alison slid into the driving seat and began to negotiate the Edinburgh traffic. She glanced at Judy sitting beside her, seeing that the headscarf was firmly in place, but pleased that sometimes there were flashes of the old Judy showing through. She'd often pulled Alison's leg about leaving things to the last minute.

★　★　★

As they drove north towards Calderlea, however, Judy began to grow quiet, though Charles Rutherford was enjoying the trip.

They were now well into winter, but it was a cold, clear, frosty morning and the countryside was lit with pale winter sunshine.

'Do you know this part of the country, Dr Rutherford?' asked Alison.

'Not nearly well enough, though I hope to remedy that,' he replied. 'And don't you think you could call me Charles? I'm on holiday, and I would like to feel a little younger.'

Alison laughed, 'Very well — Charles,' she agreed. 'I love going to Calderlea,' she went on. 'It's home to both of us, isn't it, Judy?'

But Judy made no reply. As they neared her home, she was growing more and more withdrawn, and Alison's eyes grew anxious.

She would have expected Judy to be at her best now when she needn't pretend to anyone, but instead she was quieter than she had ever been.

As they turned into the village and drove down to Hillside, Alison could feel Judy trembling beside her, but a moment later she was driving through the gateway and up the short drive to the front of the house.

Almost immediately, the door stood open in welcome and Mr and Mrs Millar came running down the steps.

Alison saw the sudden startled look in their eyes when they caught sight of Judy's changed appearance, even though they'd been well warned. Then Mrs Millar's face changed again to a quick, glad smile as she held out her arms to her daughter.

But Judy leapt from the car and turned briskly to Dr Rutherford, who was climbing out from the back.

'This is my chief, Dr Rutherford,' she introduced him. 'Charles, my — my mother and father.'

Alison could see the sudden pain in Beth Millar's eyes at Judy's rejection of her but she turned quickly and joined in welcoming their guest. They'd have to get used to the new Judy, thought Alison.

'Have you had a good journey up from London?' Mr Millar was asking. 'You came by train to Edinburgh?'

'Yes, it was very comfortable,' Charles agreed, taking out the cases while Mr Millar helped him. Alison listened to all the small talk, then a moment later they were inside the much-loved, comfortable, old house.

She saw Judy wandering about, touching old, remembered things, favourite pieces of furniture and ornaments.

'Aren't you going to take your coat off, dear?' her mother asked diffidently. 'I've prepared a meal in the dining-room.'

'I haven't much appetite, Mum,' said Judy.

'Then you can watch us eat, my girl,' Charles said cheerfully. 'Lugging these cases around is the last straw. I'm starving and so is Alison.'

They all laughed, then Judy slowly removed her coat, and pulled off the headscarf, her hand quickly pulling her hair across her forehead.

'I'll go up to my room, Mum, and — and have a wash. Perhaps I'll feel more like eating after that.'

'Very well, dear,' said Mrs Millar quietly. She caught Alison's eye, then looked away quickly.

What was wrong between Judy and her mother, Alison wondered afresh. Surely, of all people, she would have expected Judy not to mind her mother looking at her changed appearance. And she knew how much Mrs Millar loved Judy, whatever she looked like.

Yet there was an atmosphere of strain between them which was completely foreign in this household. Even Mr Millar, his good-natured face unusually pale and drawn, was a great deal more subdued than usual.

Yet it must hurt both of them to see their lovely Judy looking different,

Alison thought. They would all have to adjust.

It was left to Charles Rutherford to keep up their spirits, and Alison could see now how wise he had been in offering to bring Judy home, and in asking her to come along with them.

Over lunch he kept up an interesting conversation, bringing Alison in to help him, and some of the ice was broken. Nor did he put any taboo on the subject of their work at the research laboratory, or on Judy's accident.

'We've worked together on many projects, haven't we, Judy?' he chatted cheerfully. 'In fact, I can't think of anyone I'd rather have on my team than Dr Millar. I think there must be telepathy between us with regard to our work.'

He smiled at Judy, and Alison saw her answering smile. Was there something more in their relationship, she mused again, than the fact that they were colleagues.

Surely Charles must care deeply for

Judy when he was doing so much for her. She glanced at Charles's face, seeing the strength and good humour marked there, and feeling his dependability. Judy was lucky to have him, she thought — then she remembered Blair Walker with a small pang.

She liked Blair, too, and she knew how much he loved Judy, and Judy had also loved him. How much had it hurt her to break their engagement, and what would Blair's reaction be when he found out about Judy's accident?

★　★　★

Alison came out of her thoughts to realise that everyone was looking at her.

'I — I'm sorry,' she said, flushing. 'I was miles away. Is it pudding? If so, I'll have some, thanks.'

'You've already eaten one helping!' Judy laughed. 'You're going to get fat one day, if you go on like that.'

'She's got a long way to go,' said Charles, and there was a general lightening of the atmosphere round the table. 'Anyway, she can walk it off if she agreed with my suggestion.'

'What suggestion?' asked Alison.

'You certainly were miles away,' said Judy. 'Charles wants to walk the legs off us. As from tomorrow we tramp the hills every day, come rain or shine. He thinks the fresh air is going to . . . ' She faltered. ' . . . Is going to smooth out this — this mess!'

She pulled her hair forward again.

'But, Judy! It — it's so much better, dear!' cried Mrs Millar. 'I know it's not quite the same, but . . . '

'Yes, it is much better, isn't it!' Judy flashed, and in a moment the atmosphere seemed to crackle again.

Oh dear, thought Alison, it was going to take a long time.

'Happily you only need your feet for walking,' said Charles, 'and the sheep and cows won't mind looking at you any more than we do. So best foot forward in the morning, and maybe we could take some sandwiches, and . . . '

'A flask of tea!' put in Alison, her eyes twinkling.

This time even Judy laughed and they all relaxed again. But how slowly they had to go! thought Alison.

Next morning Charles was up before the two girls, and when Alison came downstairs, she found Mr Millar ready to go to work and all three having breakfast in the kitchen. They were talking earnestly together.

From a fragment of conversation she realised that they had been discussing the change in Judy's appearance, and Mrs Millar was wondering if she ought to take down any old photographs.

'No, leave them,' Charles told them. 'Judy mustn't try to pretend to herself that it never happened. She's got to come to terms with it.'

Mr Millar nodded slowly, and after a moment Mrs Millar, too, bowed to his opinion. Alison could see that Judy's parents were still a bit shy of her boss, but their liking and respect were beginning to grow.

'I've just been telling Dr Rutherford about some ancient monuments he might like to visit,' Mr Millar said.

'And I'll certainly take you up on it,' said Charles. 'I have sympathy for the cat who likes to explore every inch of new territory before lying in front of the fire. I like to get my bearings, too.'

Alison grinned. 'You won't find any Highlanders leaping over the hills to bash you with their claymores. Cats only inspect new territory to check up on possible dangers.'

'Charles can do it on my behalf,' said Judy, behind her. 'I don't mind going walking, but I don't want to run into Elsie Ross and her ilk. I don't fancy an inquisition at the moment.'

'Well, I'm sure you won't find Elsie leaping over the hills this morning either, dear,' her father told her, picking up his briefcase. He kissed his wife's cheek, then deliberately kissed Judy, then Alison.

'I'll see you ladies this evening.'

Alison saw that Judy had shrunk

away a little, but she pretended not to notice.

She would welcome a walk, she decided, since she often thought over her own problems while tramping the countryside, and in between worrying about Judy, her thoughts kept returning to Ken Doig, and those unreceipted bills.

The money involved was a considerable sum, and Alison's heart sank a little when she did her mental arithmetic. She would have to return the money to Ken, if Alec had spent it, and it was going to reduce her small nest-egg to minimal proportions.

She wished now that she had not been so lavish in buying new things for the flat. She would somehow have to telephone Ken and find out exactly what had happened, and that wasn't going to be easy from Calderlea.

'You're very quiet,' said Charles as they tramped along later in the morning.

'I'm out of condition!' She laughed.

'Too busy puffing and blowing.'

'Too much pudding!' Judy teased her. The breeze was blowing back her hair, and for the first time she seemed to have forgotten to pull it forward.

Alison was gradually getting used to the way Judy looked, and she decided that if only Judy could forget about her scars, they would hardly be noticed. She had been told they would fade in time.

'Your mum makes such good puddings, Jude!' Alison laughed, using an old nickname.

'Yes, she does,' said Judy, but this time there was an edge to her voice.

'Let's see if she makes good tea in a flask,' Charles suggested.

'Tea-Jenny Charles,' Judy teased, and they all sat down on a groundsheet which he had spread out.

'We go home after this,' he decided. 'This is far enough for one day, but I expect us to go twice as far within a week.'

'We'll all end up with bulging leg

muscles,' said Alison. 'But I don't mind, I feel the better for it.'

Judy said nothing. It was now time to go back home.

As soon as they opened the door, Alison could hear that Mrs Millar had a visitor and, as Charles closed the back door behind them, Judy turned almost instinctively as though she had wanted to run.

But it was too late. Mrs Millar had thrown open the sitting-room door and they all slowly walked forward into the room, where Blair Walker was rising to his feet and turning to look at Judy.

'. . . Found Wanting'

Alison paused for a moment when she saw Blair Walker rising from his seat by the fireside. Beside her, she could hear Judy's startled gasp, then her arm was gripped so tightly by Judy's slender fingers it almost hurt.

Instinctively, Alison put her hand over her friend's as they walked into the room together with Charles bringing up the rear.

'Judy!' Blair leapt to his feet and turned towards them, and before Judy had time to pull away she was in his arms, her scarred face hidden on his shoulder.

'Judy,' he repeated huskily. 'Why didn't you tell me? Why didn't you give me even a hint that you'd had this accident? To think what you've been through — and alone, too!'

Her tears threatening to spill over,

Judy tried to slide out of his arms, but Blair held on to her tightly.

'You know I'd have come to you straightaway, love,' he said. 'I'd have been there to help.'

'You couldn't have helped, Blair,' Judy said. 'My face — it's all disfigured, changed . . .'

Her head was again resting under his chin, and this time it was Blair who pushed her away and smoothed back her hair, to look at her closely.

Judy tried to turn away, but his keen eyes searched her face.

'It doesn't look so bad to me,' he said softly. 'Besides, what do appearances matter? You're still the same girl inside. I don't see why we can't get married straightaway, then I'll always be around to take care of you.'

'No!' Judy's voice was anguished and Blair drew away a little, realising that things weren't as simple as he'd hoped.

Judy bit her lip. She looked into Blair's open, frank face and saw how eager he was to show his love for her.

How kind he was to her, and how beloved he had been when she first promised to marry him.

But that seemed to have happened to her in a previous age. She felt she had lived through an eternity since then. Perhaps the scars on her face were not as bad as Blair had feared, but they were not the only scars she bore.

The others, deep inside, were even more ugly. They did not show on the surface, but she was acutely aware of them.

She could not marry Blair when she was not at peace with herself. It wouldn't be fair to him.

'No,' she whispered. 'I — I'm not ready for marriage, Blair. You'll have to give me more time.'

He released her slowly from his arms, then he looked round at Alison and Charles Rutherford.

They had tried to slip into the kitchen to give Judy and Blair more privacy, but Blair's solid frame barred the way, and from then on everything had happened so quickly.

Now Judy pulled herself together, and introduced Charles.

'Dr Rutherford is my boss at the laboratory,' she explained to Blair, who acknowledged the other man with a nod and a quick handshake. She waited for Blair to speak to him, but he turned to her again.

'We've got to talk!' he said urgently.

She shook her head, her face very white, and Alison stepped forward, concerned, Judy's general health was still too poor for such emotional situations. She saw that Blair was also looking at her anxiously.

'We've been out walking,' she explained quietly. 'We're trying to bring the roses back to Judy's cheeks. She's not awfully strong yet.'

Blair nodded, then deliberately he drew Judy to him again.

'I'm going now, love,' he said quietly, 'but I'll be back to see you. I'm glad I know what happened.'

Deliberately he kissed her scarred cheek, though Judy stepped back sharply as though she'd been stung.

'I'll show you out, Blair,' Mrs Millar said with a gentle smile. 'Thank you for coming.'

'I'll be back,' Blair promised again. 'Cheerio, Judy.'

He nodded to Alison and Charles Rutherford, then Mrs Millar closed the door quietly behind him.

Judy had sat down on one of the chairs and Alison could see that her knees were trembling.

'Are you OK?' she asked, anxiously.

For a moment Judy hesitated, then she nodded her head.

'Yes — thanks.'

'Would you like to go to bed? We can bring you up your supper on a tray,' Mrs Millar offered.

Again Judy nodded.

'Alison will help me upstairs,' she said quietly. 'Perhaps I do need a rest now.'

Alison could feel Judy's slender body

trembling beside her as she escorted her up to the bedroom, and she looked anxiously at the girl's white face.

'I'll be better in the morning,' she promised. 'I just need a good rest.'

Alison hesitated. At one time she and Judy would probably have had a heart-to-heart talk, but now it wasn't so easy.

'I'll bring up your tray,' she said quietly.

* * *

The following morning Judy came downstairs fairly late, and although she didn't feel quite so exhausted she still looked pale and drawn.

'Have you brought down your walking boots?' her mother asked. 'Or don't you feel up to it this morning?'

Judy sank into a chair. 'To be honest, I don't feel up to it this morning,' she agreed, 'but . . . '

'It would do you good to get out, dear,' Mrs Millar said gently. 'But be careful not to overdo it today, especially since Dr Rutherford and Alison are making the effort to help you.'

She smiled affectionately.

'Perhaps you could take the car for part of the way. It would be handy if you were really tired.'

A look of pain flashed across Judy's face. She had been greatly disturbed by meeting Blair and she still felt hurt and bruised.

'I know they're trying to help me, Mother,' she said, 'but you — you told Blair. I didn't want him to know just yet. Why couldn't you have helped, too, and encouraged him to leave before I got home?'

Mrs Millar flushed at the criticism.

'Well, I could hardly avoid telling him, Judy,' she said gently. 'And Blair was quite determined to wait till you returned home. I thought it was better to — to . . . '

'Warn him?' Judy asked, her hand going up again to her face.

'To let him know that you've suffered

a great deal of pain, my dear,' Mrs Millar went on. 'I thought he was entitled to know.'

Alison bit her lip, looking from one to the other. Previously there had been a strained atmosphere between them, but now it was turning into open hostility on Judy's part.

Then Charles walked in breezily.

'Come on,' he encouraged, 'put your best foot forward, Judy — no, I should say 'better' foot, shouldn't I? I mean, you haven't got three!'

In spite of herself, Judy managed a smile and Charles took her arm.

'Where's your scarf, Alison?' he asked. 'The wind's pretty icy.'

'I'll get it,' Alison said, and ran up to her room. When she came down, Charles and Judy were already waiting at the gate, and she saw that Mrs Millar was looking out at them, her expression anxious.

Alison hurried out to join the other two though her thoughts were on the older woman. It seemed to her that the gulf was widening between her and Judy.

The walk that day was not a success. The wind was too strong and it barred Charles and Alison from holding any conversation, so that Judy's silence seemed even more marked than usual.

She had pulled her woollen cap over her ears and the wind seemed to burn the soft new tissue on her scarred cheek.

'I think I'd like to go home,' she said at length, 'and have a bit of a lie down. I don't feel like myself at all.'

'OK, Judy,' Alison agreed. 'Do you want me to get the car?'

'No, I'll be fine,' Judy assured her. 'I'll try to walk further tomorrow.'

'Maybe I've been pushing you too much,' Charles said contritely. 'I'm sorry, Judy.'

'No,' she said quickly. 'No, you've been very good. It's just that — that I'm still a little tired, but I'm stronger on the whole.'

Charles nodded, though he was

feeling slightly disappointed. The days of his holiday were passing and he had hoped to see a daily improvement in Judy. It was discouraging to see her slipping back a little.

Mrs Millar made no comment when Judy went back to bed shortly after lunch. She had pecked at her food, but she promised to eat something later if Alison cooked it for her.

Alison went into the kitchen to help Mrs Millar with the washing-up. Although her thoughts had mainly been on Judy, she'd also had one other worry which was growing larger and larger so that she was beginning to lose sleep over it.

She couldn't forget the unpaid bills belonging to Ken Doig, which had been found among Alec's papers. Ken had given Alec the money to pay them.

What had happened to that money, she wondered. What on earth could have happened to it?

Ken could not be expected to write off that sort of loss, so she must repay it, every penny, if she found no trace of the actual money among Alec's things.

Absently Alison quietly washed through her tea-towel, then she turned to Mrs Millar.

'Could I possibly make a telephone call?' she asked. 'It — it's rather private.'

'But of course, dear,' said Mrs Millar. 'Just go ahead. I'll see you're not disturbed.'

'Thank you,' Alison said gratefully. The sooner she got this matter sorted out, the better.

★   ★   ★

When Alison got through to Ken's number, he asked her to hang on for a little while as he was in the middle of an urgent bit of business. She could feel her nerves tightening with anxiety before he came to pick up the receiver again.

'Sorry to keep you waiting, Alison,' he said. 'I had to sign for a delivery of goods and the van driver was double-parked. What can I do for you?'

'Well, I'm really worried about those two bills I found among Alec's papers, Ken,' she said. 'Did you pick them up from Ian's place?'

She heard his quick intake of breath and his voice was suddenly rather diffident.

'Yes, I picked them up, Alison. Er, you didn't mention anything about them to Ian, I suppose?'

'No, of course not,' she said, 'but I'd like to know more about them myself. Why do you ask, Ken?'

'Oh, nothing important,' he said, though she could hear the slightly strained note in his voice. 'Ian's inclined to assume that he knows everything at times, that's all. He jumps to conclusions.'

Alison hesitated. She was too anxious about the bills to discuss Ian Thomson.

'Did you give Alec the money to pay those bills, Ken?' she asked, bluntly.

Again he hesitated. 'Well, yes, I did,

Alison,' he told her.

'And he hasn't paid them?'

'No, apparently not.'

Alison began to feel sick at heart. It was every bit as bad as she had feared.

'I'll make sure you get your money back, Ken,' she promised.

'No, Alison!' he said quickly. 'There's no need for that just yet. Maybe you'll find the money when you look through the rest of Alec's things. There wasn't a great deal of time. I mean . . . '

Ken's voice tailed off miserably. Whatever he said seemed destined to hurt Alison.

'I'll come home straightaway, Ken,' she decided. 'I won't be able to rest until I get to the bottom of this. I'll be in touch with you as soon as I get back to the flat.'

'Are you sure you won't upset yourself, Alison?' Ken's voice was anxious. 'Ian Thomson said you were pretty upset when you called in at the shop. I think he blamed me.'

'No, I'll be OK, Ken. Don't worry

from that point of view. Look, I've got to go now. I'll be in touch.'

'There's no hurry at all,' Ken said. 'In fact, I've got to go away for a day or two.'

'I'm still returning to Edinburgh,' Alison said firmly. 'I want to get this settled.'

For a long moment, Alison stood motionless after she had hung up the telephone, her thoughts crowding in on her. Judy wasn't quite so well, but she felt she could not put her whole energy into helping her friend while the problem of the missing money hung over her.

From the direction of the sitting-room she could hear the low murmur of voices as Mrs Millar and Charles talked together. Slowly Alison moved forward and opened the door.

'Oh, there you are, Alison,' Mrs Millar said brightly. 'Come and sit down by the fire.'

'Only for a moment,' Alison replied, and Charles guided her to a seat, his eyes concerned when he noticed the nervous twisting of her fingers.

'I've got to go back to Edinburgh straightaway, Mrs Millar,' she said. 'I'm sorry, but I'm afraid it's essential.'

'Oh dear, I hope there's nothing wrong,' Mrs Millar said with concern.

'No, it's just a small business matter,' Alison said as lightly as she could. 'But it has to be dealt with quickly.'

'I'm coming with you.'

Alison turned round to see Judy standing in the doorway in her russet-brown housecoat and slippers, but Alison noticed that her hair was again carefully combed forward over her face.

Judy still could not relax over her appearance, even with her own family.

'Oh, Judy, are you sure you're well enough?' her mother asked.

'I travelled all the way from London,' Judy said briefly. 'I can surely make the short journey to Edinburgh.'

'But — but Dr Rutherford . . . '

'I'm afraid my holiday is over in any

case, Mrs Millar,' Charles said quickly. 'I'll have to go back to London.'

Alison looked from one to the other.

'I know you've got your project to do,' Judy went on, turning to her, 'but I promise not to get in the way. At least I'm well enough to attend to my own needs.'

'All right, Judy. I'll be glad of your company.' Alison caught Mrs Millar's eye and saw the fleeting look of pain on the older woman's face.

'Suppose we leave first thing in the morning?' she suggested, glancing at the clock. That would give Mrs Millar time to get used to the idea and she would see to it that Charles Rutherford had plenty of time to catch his train.

Alison forced herself to be patient, even though her whole instinct was to leap into the car straightaway and hurry home to the flat.

Mrs Millar was obviously relieved.

'Get a good rest then, Judy,' she advised. 'Then you'll feel more able to

143

travel back to Edinburgh in the morning.'

*　*　*

That evening after supper the house was very quiet as Alison sat down by the fireside. Mr Millar had taken Dr Rutherford along to the church hall to see an exhibition of photography, and Mrs Millar came to sit down beside Alison.

'I'm glad you postponed your return home until tomorrow, Alison,' she said quietly. 'I've been wanting to talk to you before you left.'

Alison laid aside her knitting.

'Is it about Judy?' she asked gently.

Mrs Millar sighed and nodded, a look of anguish on her face.

'I know it must be obvious to you that there's something very wrong between us. It's all my fault, I'm afraid. I — I let her down just when she needed me most.'

'You let Judy down!' Alison cried. 'I

can't believe that.'

'Oh, but I did,' Mrs Millar went on. 'Shortly after the accident, Walter and I travelled to London to see her in hospital. We had been told what had happened of course, but — but I was quite unprepared for the sight of Judy at that time.'

She sighed.

'Walter said that I was tired after the journey and all the upset of learning about the accident.' She stared into the fire, and Alison could see the tears gathering in her eyes.

'It must have been a terrible experience,' the girl said, reaching out to take the older woman's hand. 'I don't think you should blame yourself for anything.'

'I should have acted more thoughtfully, Alison, tired or not. There's no excuse. We arrived at the hospital and we were allowed in to see Judy straightaway.' Mrs Millar's voice trembled.

'She was in a private room and

. . . Alison, you didn't see her immediately after it happened. You didn't see how badly she was injured, and how much she was suffering.'

She wiped away a tear.

'The plastic surgeons have really done wonders for her, but at that time, seeing her so suddenly, looking the way she did, well, I made a fool of myself. I let her see how appalled I was at the sight of her and I think I said things to Walter — things that Judy could hear. I said it — it just wasn't Judy . . . '

Her voice shuddered into silence and Alison sat still, knowing very well how hurt Judy must have been. Yet it was the great love which Mrs Millar felt for Judy that had made her react so violently to the sight of those disfiguring burns.

'She was depending on me for comfort and reassurance, and I didn't give it to her,' Mrs Millar went on after a moment. 'I was put to the test and found wanting.'

Her voice was suddenly bitter against herself.

'So how can I blame Judy for — for being angry with me now? She must have felt so hurt, and so alone. She should have been able to turn freely to the one person she could really depend on — me, her mother. Yet I let her down.'

Mrs Millar was now weeping quietly and Alison took her in her arms to comfort her. It would do her good to cry.

She had never been the type of woman who shed tears easily, and she had probably bottled up all her grief since she had first heard about Judy's accident.

But there was also uneasiness in Alison's heart. She knew Judy, and she could not think of anything more calculated to hurt her than listening to her mother's unguarded words when she set eyes on Judy's scarred face.

No wonder the girl had now lost confidence in her own appearance . .

'We'll all have to be very patient, Mrs Millar,' Alison said softly. 'It isn't going to be at all easy.'

'Perhaps one day I'll be able to make her see how deeply sorry and ashamed I feel,' Mrs Millar said. 'Perhaps she'll find it in her heart to forgive me.'

'I'm sure she will when she feels better.'

'I can only hope and pray. I felt you ought to know the truth, though, dear. You must have wondered . . . '

'I'm so glad you told me,' Alison told her. 'If I can ever do anything to put things right, then, believe me, I will.'

★ ★ ★

The following morning, Alison drove Judy and Charles back to Edinburgh. Judy hadn't bothered to pack many clothes, but there was a sense of urgency about her, as though she couldn't wait to leave Calderlea.

Alison squeezed Mrs Millar's hand after she had kissed the older woman goodbye. Her heart ached for her, and she smiled reassuringly.

'I'll telephone often,' she whispered. 'Don't worry, I'll look after Judy.'

Dr Rutherford was also sorry to leave, and he shook hands warmly with Judy's parents.

'I've had a lovely break,' he assured them. 'I shan't take kindly to being back at work in London.'

'Come again some day,' Mrs Millar invited.

How lonely she looks, Alison thought, as Mrs Millar stood in the doorway and waved them away. Alison, too, felt strangely lonely after she and Judy saw Charles on to the London train.

'We're going to miss Charles,' she said to Judy as they returned to the flat. She had to walk slowly for Judy's sake, though she longed to run all the way so she could quickly begin her search through Alec's belongings.

Alison had picked up her post and the key of the flat from Ian Thomson's shop, but Ian had been busy with a customer, and she told him she would see him later.

Ian lived above the shop during the week, but at weekends he travelled home to stay with his parents in Hawick where Mr Thomson was employed in one of the banks.

Alison had seen his eyes lighting up at the sight of her, but nothing else seemed to matter other than her desire to find the money for Ken.

'You're going too fast, Alison.' Judy's breathless voice broke into her thoughts.

'Oh, sorry.' Alison's pace slowed. They should have taken the car to the station from the flat, she thought a trifle irritably, but she felt the traffic was a handicap when a short distance was involved. Now every step seemed like a mile.

'Are you in a desperate hurry, or something?' Judy asked.

Again Alison narrowed her stride. 'Well, I have to look for something . . . '

'Can I help?'

'No. I — I have to look through Alec's personal things.'

'Oh, I see,' Judy said, suddenly aware that Alison, too, was living through a difficult time. She took Alison's arm.

'I'm sorry,' she said, her voice warm with sympathy. 'Do you miss him very much?'

'Yes,' Alison said, rather briefly. 'But I've got to find something for Ken Doig. It's probably among Alec's personal things, and the quicker I get on with it, the better.'

Back in the flat Judy decided that she would make tea to allow Alison time to go through Alec's papers. The fire had died down but Alison forgot about trying to keep it going.

Her one thought was to go through Alec's belongings. She had put everything away when it was returned to her after the accident and she had been unable to lay a finger on his personal things because of the heart-ache she felt every time she saw his well-worn possessions.

Now, however, her fears and urgency were driving her to handle every single object.

She emptied out his briefcase again, looking at paper after paper, just in case she spotted something she had missed the previous time. But there was nothing which gave any clue as to where the money had gone.

Then she began to search through Alec's more personal things — his wallet, the watch she had given him for Christmas, the signet ring she had bought when they became engaged, and the cheap ball-point pen he had bought after losing his expensive one.

Alison discarded them one by one, then she began to search through his clothing. He had quite a number of suits and casual clothes, and she found a penknife he had 'mislaid.'

For a moment her eyes misted with memory when she recalled how diligently she had searched for it at the time. However, after that find, each pocket was completely empty except for one or two handkerchiefs. There was no sign of Ken's money.

Alison laid Alec's best suit aside, then picked up his overcoat. Gently she slid her hand into the inside pocket, and her fingers tightened as they curled round a small package.

She drew it out, seeing that it was a sealed envelope. With trembling fingers Alison undid the envelope and lifted out a familiar velvet box. She opened the lid, then lifted out the beautiful bracelet which had belonged to her grandmother.

Alison stared at it almost stupidly. It had been cleaned and polished, and the diamonds, set in gold, shone with intense brilliance. But Alec had pawned it, she remembered. He had pawned it . . .

Then she knew she was looking at the explanation for the disappearance of Ken's money. Alec must have redeemed the bracelet as soon as he could. No doubt he'd expected to pay the bills out of his salary.

It was so like him, she thought, sinking to her knees. Oh, Alec! His first thought had been to get the bracelet back for her.

Suddenly she was sobbing her heart out, even as she clutched the bracelet to her heart. Alec had always known how much she loved it, and now she wept out her love for him for getting it back for her.

Nevertheless, he shouldn't have used Ken's money, Alison thought, as she calmed herself. That must be paid back immediately. She had no idea where it was going to come from, but she must pay it back somehow.

Alison went to find her savings bankbook. If she drew out every penny and added it to the money she had in her ordinary account, there would be just enough to pay Ken back again.

'Tea's ready,' Judy said, coming to find her.

Alison looked at her blankly. 'Oh,' she said. 'Oh yes, tea . . . ' She glanced at the clock. 'I'll be back as soon as I can, Judy,' she promised. 'I've just got to go out for a moment.'

A moment later, she rushed out of the flat.

Making Progress

In later months, Alison often looked back to that moment when she found her bracelet in Alec's coat pocket. It had a dream-like quality, as had her visit to the bank in order to draw out the money to pay Ken, and she had no clear idea as to the details of that afternoon.

The large sum which she drew out left her account very low, but Alison didn't care. Ken Doig was away on business, she remembered, but that was all to the good. She was in no mood to argue with him if he wanted to be difficult about accepting the money. So she quickly put the notes into an envelope and made her way to Ken's office.

Anna Bennett, Ken's secretary, looked up with a welcoming smile when Alison walked into the office.

'Oh, hello, Mrs Drummond,' she greeted. 'I'm afraid Mr Doig is away at the moment . . . '

'I know,' Alison said, smiling as naturally as she could, though her face felt stiff with nerves. She saw that Anna was looking at her closely, so she lost no time in producing the envelope.

'This is some money I had to hand in for Mr Doig,' she said evenly. 'I wonder if you could put it in the bank, please? It's quite a large sum and I don't think either of us should be responsible for it.'

Anna took the money.

'No, I know what you mean, Mrs Drummond. I'll see to it straightaway. Er, does Mr Doig know about this? I mean . . . '

'I'll leave him a note, if you let me have some scrap paper,' Alison said. 'But in fact, he does know about it.'

'That's fine,' Anna said, satisfied.

A moment later Alison was back in the street. Now that she was free of the money, she felt strangely relieved, but the feeling of unreality persisted.

She had put the box containing her bracelet into her handbag. Now she opened the bag a little, peeping in to make sure she hadn't dreamed it all, and that Alec really had got the bracelet back for her.

It must have been one of the last things he did, she realised, a sob rising in her throat. Recovering the bracelet must have been one of the last things he did before . . . before the accident.

Her head throbbed as she climbed the stairs once again to the flat, and her footsteps began to drag so that it was almost an effort to reach the door and let herself in with her key. She was vaguely aware of Judy in the kitchen, and her cry of pleasure now that Alison had returned.

'Did you get all your business attended to?' Judy was talking brightly. 'What about tea, Alison? Would you like me to make you a cup now? Alison!'

Judy had come into the sitting-room from the kitchen, and she stopped short when she saw Alison slumped in a chair, her handbag dangling from her fingers.

She was still wearing her outdoor coat and her face was so white that Judy's heart bounded with shock. Alison seemed to be looking straight through her, her eyes glazed.

'Alison!' she cried. 'What is it? What's the matter?'

Judy knelt down in front of Alison's chair. She was about to take her handbag but Alison clutched it almost convulsively.

'No,' she whispered. 'No. I want to keep it.'

'I wasn't going to take it from you,' Judy said, her alarm growing. Alison looked as though she had received a great shock.

'Look, I've built up the fire and it's lovely and bright. Just let me take your coat off, Alison, then I'll get you something hot to drink.'

Swiftly Judy removed the coat, allowing Alison to keep hold of her bag.

Then quickly she went into the kitchen and made a cup of hot tea, to which she added a drop of brandy.

Alison had hardly moved when Judy returned to the lounge and knelt again in front of her chair.

'Here, Alison,' she said. 'Drink this. It should make you feel better.'

She had to coax a little more, but eventually Alison drank the hot tea, then she began to cough and a moment later she was again crying helplessly while Judy put her arms round her to comfort her.

'Oh, Alison,' she said, her own tears not far away. 'Whatever has happened to upset you like this? What is it? Isn't there anything I can do?'

★   ★   ★

Gradually Alison's sobs subsided and she reached into her handbag for a clean handkerchief, her hands once again caressing her precious jewellery box. Her fingers closed over it and she drew it out and showed it to Judy.

'It — it was finding this,' she said chokily. 'Oh, Judy, if only you knew what it meant to me. If only you understood how I feel . . . '

'Try me,' said Judy, as she stared at the lovely bracelet. 'This is your family heirloom, I remember you showed it to me once or twice. It's really beautiful, Alison, and it must be very valuable these days.'

'It is.' Alison nodded. 'But it's so much more valuable than I ever realised. I — I suppose I'd better tell you the whole story. You see, a week or two before Alec died, he left me . . . '

'Alison!' Judy cried, her eyes wide with disbelief.

'It's true,' Alison nodded. 'We — we had an awful row, Judy, over his new job with Ken. He always seemed to have some new scheme afoot, and I helped him to get them off the ground time after time. Then, of course — they failed . . . '

Alison's voice tailed off, and she

wiped her eyes with her handkerchief.

'But when Alec came home and told me he was going in with Ken, I just rebelled. I think I was terrified he would harm Ken's business in some way by his own incompetence. Oh, I don't know — maybe it was just the last straw — but I refused to help him financially, even though I could have done it, Judy. Can you imagine how I felt about that later?'

'Oh, Alison,' said Judy, in a low voice. She could see the anguish on her friend's face as the tears started up again.

'So he left me,' Alison continued after a moment, 'but he took my bracelet with him. He left a note to say he was going to pawn it to raise part of the money he needed to go in with Ken.'

Alison gulped and drank a little more of her tea.

'At the time I was hurt. Then, later, after Alec was killed, it felt as though I had put more value on my bracelet than on Alec's life. I felt I could have given him a hundred bracelets, if only I had them.'

She sighed.

'I felt mean, horribly mean, for not supporting him and for being so upset that he had taken my bracelet. Yet at the same time I was hurt. Can you understand that, Judy?'

'Of course I can. You couldn't foresee what would happen. But how have you managed to get it back?'

'About a week ago — maybe a few days longer — Ken asked me to look through Alec's papers for some bills he had asked Alec to pay. He had also given Alec the money for the bills. But he found out that the bills hadn't been paid and it seemed as though the money had gone missing.'

Alison sighed, and Judy waited, saying nothing, though she had grasped Alison's hand tightly.

'I looked through all Alec's papers, but there was just nothing to account for the disappearance of the money. When I came back from Calderlea this morning, I could hardly wait to go through everything again.'

'I knew you were busy,' Judy said, 'but I didn't realise . . . '

'I had almost given up,' Alison said rather tiredly, her eyes now swollen with weeping. 'Then I put my hand into the pocket of his best coat and found this box with my bracelet in it. It's pretty obvious now where the money went.

'Oh, Judy, can't you see what he did? He got my bracelet back for me. He still cared about me, even though he had walked out. His first thought was for me. Can you understand how that makes me feel?' Alison sobbed.

'Of course I can,' Judy said warmly. 'It means that Alec must have loved you very deeply.'

'I feel I've been given the world. Yet none of it's real when I don't have Alec.'

'But you do have him,' Judy cried quickly. 'You know now that you had never really lost him, even though he had left you.

'So if you were hurt by thinking he'd walked out on you, surely the finding of the bracelet should heal your heart, Alison? Doesn't it help you to know he never stopped loving you?'

Alison's sobs subsided again.

'Yes, you're right,' she replied slowly. 'Perhaps that's why I was so keen to pay the money back to Ken straightaway. I drew it all out of my Savings Account. I just didn't care how much was left . . . '

Judy looked at her quickly. Did that mean that Alison's finances were now a bit low?

'That's the spirit,' was all she said.

'I took it round to Ken's office,' Alison went on, 'and gave it to his secretary. It'll be in the bank by now. I feel as though I've really got my bracelet — and Alec — back,' she added softly. 'You're quite right, Judy.'

★   ★   ★

Judy again bit her lip. In a strange sort of way she knew exactly how Alison felt, but she also felt that Alison needed to see it all in the right perspective.

She could now remember Alec with nothing but love, but she also needed to remember that she had to pick up the pieces of her life again, and not be obsessed by what had happened. Perhaps her encouraging words had not helped Alison in the right direction.

'Well it must have been a great relief to pay the money back,' she said rather more briskly. 'And don't go worrying about money either. You know I can always help you there.'

Alison nodded, leaning back in her chair. Now that she had told Judy, she felt a strange sense of peace.

'I've got a chicken casserole in the oven,' said Judy. 'You rest there for a little while and I'll serve it up. Let's just have it sitting here at the fire, instead of being civilised and eating at the dining-table. How about it?'

'Just a small portion for me,' Alison agreed. 'I don't really feel hungry.'

'You made me eat when I didn't feel

like it,' Judy said, smiling. 'Now it's your turn to do as you're told!'

As she went into the kitchen, her own words seemed to echo in her ears. It seemed ages ago since Alison had sought her out and practically forced her to get on with her life again. How wrapped up in herself she had been!

She hadn't even noticed that Alison had problems of her own, and Judy experienced a queer sense of shame that she had become so introverted. In fact, the past hour or two was the first time she had forgotten about herself since the accident.

⋆　⋆　⋆

Deliberately she walked over to the kitchen mirror and touched her face, gazing at her own reflection. She still looked awful, she thought. She doubted whether she'd ever come to terms with her changed appearance, but in an odd sort of way it had done her good to become involved with Alison's

167

problems for a while, instead of her own.

How ironic, she thought, that Alison had been trying so hard to get her to come to terms with herself, yet she had only made the first step when Alison's own troubles became too great to bear.

Judy found a dainty tray-cloth and pretty dinner plates and forks. If they were going to picnic round the fire, they might as well do it in style, she thought, with a sudden lift of the heart.

Picking up the tray, she carried it through to the lounge.

'We'll watch the news on TV,' she said, switching it on. 'I fancy a quiet evening, don't you?'

Alison nodded, smiling gently.

It was like old times — almost.

Next morning Alison was still tired and her head ached a little as she began to sort out the work she had to do.

She was behind schedule and her sense of urgency, added to her nervousness about tackling the job, made her make a mess of her first few drawings.

One by one they were torn from the drawing-board and thrown into the wastepaper basket with increasing frustration.

Judy had offered to attend to the household chores, and Alison was more than grateful. She had often been used to working with Alec prowling up and down the flat and the sounds of movement were quite comforting.

'Have a break for coffee,' Judy suggested at her elbow, 'then try again. You always used to say it took you an hour or two to get worked in.'

'I know,' Alison said ruefully. 'But I'm running out of materials. I'll have to go to Ian's.'

'I'll go for you,' Judy offered, then she caught her breath. She had offered without thought, then she realised that it would be the first time she had gone out alone since her accident. She felt nervous in case people stared at her.

But already Alison was accepting her offer gratefully.

'Oh, Judy, would you?' she asked. 'I'll write down the list. You know, this little break has done me the world of good. I really feel I can start again.'

Judy nodded. She could hardly change her mind now. While Alison wrote out the list, she slowly put on her coat and scarf, pulling it forward as usual over her face. Alison hardly noticed, however, as she handed Judy the list.

'I have a monthly account with Ian,' she said, 'so it goes on the slate. No need to take any money.'

'Fine,' Judy said, picking up a shopping bag.

'Oh, and can you return these two art magazines Ian lent me?' Alison asked. 'I've been forgetting to take them back for ages.'

Judy walked briskly towards Ian's shop. The Edinburgh streets were busy with tourists but Judy scarcely looked at the throng of people. She was primarily concerned to reach the sanctuary of Ian's shop, where she could relax once more. It was alarming to be out on her own.

Judy pushed open the door and remembered to watch out for the step. A tall, middle-aged man was talking to Ian at the counter. He was discussing the Royal Academy Summer Exhibition earlier in the year and how many of the paintings had been very bold in the use of colour.

Judy hung back a little, transferring the magazines to her other hand. One of them slipped from her fingers and fell to the floor. Immediately the tall man stooped to retrieve it for her, even as Judy, herself, bent down, her scarf slipping from her head.

For a long moment they stared at one another, then Judy saw a change coming over the man's expression. It was a look almost of recognition. His eyes searched her face.

She coloured vividly and adjusted the scarf again, yet as he turned to leave the shop, Judy had the odd feeling that he hardly noticed her scars. He was looking at her as a person, she thought instinctively, not at her injured face, and there was something in his gaze which she didn't quite understand.

'Goodbye then, Mr Neill. I'll see you again sometime,' Ian was saying cheerfully.

' 'Bye, Mr Thomson.' The man paused for a moment, looking again at Judy, then the shop door clanged and she turned back to Ian.

'Well, hello, Judy,' he greeted her. 'I can't tell you how good it is to see you. Isn't Alison with you today?'

'She's too busy, Ian,' Judy explained. 'I've brought a list of supplies for you to make up. It's that new project, you know.'

'Yes, that's right. It's a demanding piece of work.'

Ian studied the shopping list and began to make up the order, thanking Judy for bringing his magazines back.

They had known one another a long time, Judy thought, as she relaxed and wandered round Ian's shop.

'Are you staying long in Edinburgh?' he asked, after they had chatted amicably for a short while.

'Until Alison throws me out!' Judy laughed, then her eyes sobered. 'I don't know, Ian. I've no real plans at the moment, except to live each day as it comes.'

'A good philosophy,' Ian agreed, as he handed over the parcel. 'Cheerio, Judy. Remember me to Alison.'

'Cheerio,' she echoed, and a moment later she was again in the street. Somehow her thoughts went back to the tall man who had looked at her so searchingly, and again she could visualise the almost startled look in his eyes as they held hers.

Who was he, she wondered. Her thoughts were so full of the older man that she was climbing the stairs at the flat almost before she knew it.

Yet it was Judy who was tired when she let herself in with her key. This time it was Alison who had prepared a light lunch for them, and Judy who sat down to it gratefully.

Another milestone had been overcome, she thought. She had managed to go out into the street on her own. She had made the first step forward, but the effort had tired her, and she was glad to sit down with a book that afternoon, as Alison once again applied herself to her work.

This time her work began to go well and she worked solidly all afternoon. She felt stiff and cramped when eventually she laid her painting materials aside. She wearily wiped her hands with a turpentine rag but her heart felt more contented than it had for some time.

'Well?' Judy asked. 'I've been almost afraid to move. How's it going?'

'Fine,' Alison replied rather cautiously. She believed, within herself, that it might be the best thing she had ever done.

'I need a bath now,' she said to Judy, her hands smoothing down her stained overall.

'And I'll have to get used to the smell of paint and turpentine!' Judy laughed.

Alison nodded more soberly. That was exactly what Alec had once said.

* * *

It was two evenings later when the bell of the flat shrilled loudly just as the girls had settled down for a quiet evening. Alison had suggested that Judy accompany her to a meeting of the Arts Society, which interested her, but Judy did not feel up to going out socially just yet.

'Let's go for a picnic on Saturday then,' Alison suggested. 'Somewhere quiet. It isn't good to stay in too much.'

'Well, maybe,' Judy said, rather vaguely. She still didn't care to go out very much. 'It's so comfortable here this evening. I do like this flat, Alison, now that I'm used to it. Oh, bother! Who can that be?'

Alison heaved herself up from the chair to answer the ring at the bell, though she was slightly taken aback when she saw Ken Doig on the doorstep. She hadn't expected him to be back home just yet.

'Hello, Alison,' he greeted her. 'Can I come in?'

'Yes, of course, Ken,' said Alison, showing him through to the lounge, where Judy had risen to her feet.

'Hello, Judy,' Ken said easily. 'My word, that's a nice fire. You girls certainly like your creature comforts!'

Judy's laugh rang out.

'Well, you know us,' she said. 'We should have been born on a tropical island.'

'You poor, cold things,' Ken said with mock sympathy, so that both girls laughed again. It really was like old times, thought Alison.

'I'll make us some coffee and sandwiches,' she said. 'Judy and I have just been pushing one another to go and make supper.'

'Well, you've just won — this time,' said Judy, rising to her feet. 'You talk to

Ken and I'll do it.'

Ken's eyes followed Judy, then he turned to Alison.

'There was no need . . . ' he began.

'There was every need,' Alison said quickly. 'I know what you're going to say, Ken, but maybe when I explain . . . '

Swiftly she explained to Ken as many of the facts as she wanted him to know, and also explained a little about the bracelet.

'It's so like Alec,' she ended sadly. 'And I do hope you understand, Ken. He'd never have used the money like that if he hadn't believed he'd soon be able to pay those bills himself. He was probably desperate to redeem the bracelet for my sake. That's why I felt I must return the money to you straight-away.'

Ken's brown eyes had hardly left her face, and now he nodded slowly. He had arrived, determined to make Alison accept the money back again until she felt free to pay him without any hardship, but now his admiration for her integrity knew no bounds.

Alec Drummond's ethics had taken a bit of understanding, but Alison had always understood him very well. Now it was his turn to understand Alison and to accept the money straightaway.

'I know what you mean,' he said gently. 'I can only thank you very much for clearing it all up.'

Alison relaxed and her eyes brimmed with laughter as Ken rose to help Judy with the tea tray and they bickered amicably over setting it out on the table.

'You once set out a wee table like that at your birthday party, Judy, and I succeeded in knocking it over. I'll lift over that bigger table, if you don't mind!'

'Do you mean to say you haven't changed in twenty years, Ken Doig?' asked Judy.

'Is it twenty? You were at least nine at the time.'

'You know exactly how old I am,'

Judy said, laughing. 'You're three years older.'

'Twenty-eight,' Ken said ruefully. 'Less of that sugar, Judy, or·I'll get a paunch.'

The girls laughed helplessly, since Ken was tall and thin.

'And still a bachelor,' Judy teased.

For a moment Ken's eyes flickered towards Alison, then back to Judy.

'Still a bachelor,' he agreed quietly.

'He's too busy expanding that business of his!' Alison laughed. 'He becomes a different person when he starts to show you over his fine premises.'

'It's something to be proud of,' Judy said, 'though he once wanted to drive a fire engine, if I remember.'

'An engine driver, surely,' Alison said.

'No, it was a fire engine,' Judy retorted. 'He got a fire engine for his birthday.'

'Which one? I don't remember,' Ken asked.

'Twenty-first!' Judy replied, and he

aimed a cushion at her.

'Behave, both of you, and eat your sandwiches,' Alison said, her eyes dancing, and soon they were busily remembering many incidents from their childhood.

Judy grew a little quiet again as she thought about how her own life had turned out. For a while she watched the other two, then she threw off her dull mood and poured more coffee.

It was quite late when Ken eventually rose to go, and Alison saw him to the door. Judy was collecting cups and saucers when she returned to the sitting-room.

'Well, that was a nice evening,' Alison said. 'It really was just like old times.'

'Not quite,' said Judy, and Alison's face sobered.

'I don't mean me — I mean Ken,' Judy said, reading her mind.

'Ken?'

'Yes. He's falling in love with you, isn't he, Alison?'

'It's All My Fault'

Alison stared at Judy, the colour slowly creeping into her cheeks. Surely she was joking! But Judy's eyes were steady as she regarded her friend.

'Don't be silly,' Alison said, laughing a little with embarrassment. 'You do allow your imagination to run away with you at times, Judy!'

'It's not imagination. They say the onlooker sees most of the game, and it isn't very difficult to see into Ken's heart. I tell you, Alison, he's falling in love with you.'

Alison sat down, a sick feeling in her heart. She wanted to be angry with Judy for spoiling the end of a lovely evening, but at the same time she realised that if Judy was correct, then it was better that she knew. Then she wouldn't unwittingly encourage Ken.

'You — you're really sure, Judy?' she

181

asked in a low voice.

'I'm sure,' Judy said firmly. 'He's very nice, Alison,' she added, as an afterthought.

'I know,' Alison said rather wretchedly. 'That makes it worse, but it would all be such a waste of time for him, Judy. I'm never likely to feel that way about him. For me there was only Alec, and now that he's gone I — well — I just couldn't fall in love again.'

Judy looked at Alison. The soft light brought a glow of colour to her fair hair, and her dark eyes shone against the creamy pallor of her skin. She had always admired Alison's looks. Even more so now that her own had changed.

For a moment Judy's eyes were shadowed, then she put the thought behind her. She was slowly learning that, as each day passed, she grew more accustomed to her new way of life, and could take more interest in what was happening around her. That seemed to be enough at the moment.

Alison's future, for example, was just one such interest.

'You're still very young and attractive, Alison,' Judy said quietly. 'You have a long life ahead of you. Perhaps it's too soon to think about sharing it with anyone else just yet, but I don't think you should just accept the fact that you'll live the rest of your life on your own.'

'I have my work, Judy,' Alison murmured after a long silence. 'That's all I ask. I don't want to think about anything else just yet.'

'OK,' Judy said, with a quick change of mood as she rose to her feet. 'I forgot you're a working girl, so bed for you, this instant! I'll just clear up these few dishes, then see that everything is made safe for the night. See you in the morning.'

''Night, Judy,' Alison said wearily. Neverthless Judy's words about Ken were still uppermost in her mind as she lay down to sleep. She didn't want to hurt him. Surely Judy must be wrong!

183

The following morning Alison looked rather pale and tired when she crawled out of bed. She put on her dressing-gown and slippers and padded through to the kitchen where Judy already had breakfast cooking.

'That coffee smells good,' Alison said. 'I forgot to open my window last night, and I've given myself a head-ache.'

Judy looked at her and nodded.

'I've put the water heater on, so you'll be able to have a bath shortly. I expect it's work again straightaway?'

'Oh yes, I do want to get on with that new set of paintings. There was a bit which wasn't quite right, but last night — just before I got to sleep — I suddenly realised where I was going wrong. I'm sure I'll manage it better this morning.'

Judy smiled a little, looking at her friend speculatively. Alison was cer-tainly dedicated when it came to her work. She seemed to be growing more wrapped up in it every day.

'There's the post,' she said, as they heard the sound of letters dropping on to the mat in the hall. 'I'll get it.'

Judy returned a moment later and handed Alison most of the mail, keeping one letter for herself.

'This is for me,' she said slowly, adding almost reluctantly. 'It's from Blair.'

Alison looked up, but this time Judy's face was impassive. She took a great deal of interest in Alison's affairs, but she was inclined to keep rather quiet about her own!

Rather nervously, Judy looked at the letter from Blair. He hadn't been able to take no for an answer, she thought, and he had made it very clear that he intended to stay in her life.

Blair expected her to be just the same despite her changed face, but sometimes she was afraid she just wasn't the same person. Sometimes she was afraid that the accident had changed her in every way, and not just in appearance.

Slowly she opened the letter and

began to read, seeing that the address was a hotel in London, and as she continued to read, her heart jerked with shock. Blair was on his way to Alaska!

I'm sorry I couldn't get in touch before I left Calderlea, Judy, he wrote, *but the chance of this job came up rather hurriedly. I'm actually joining a team who are investigating mineral deposits in Alaska.*

I had to decide quickly whether or not I wanted to go, as a member of the team had to drop out at the last moment. It's a permananent job and I expect to be in Alaska for quite a while.

It's too good a chance to miss, you know. It's what I've always wanted to do.

It'll be quite an adventure to live in Alaska, and at last I'll have some really interesting work to do. I'm looking forward to it.

Sorry I haven't managed to come

to Edinburgh to say a proper goodbye, but, as I said, everything's happened so quickly.

Take care of yourself.

All my love, Blair.

Judy read then re-read the letter, frowning slightly with concentration and, as it began to sink in, she sat down again at the kitchen table feeling strangely depressed by Blair's news.

She'd broken off their engagement, but somehow she'd been aware of him always in the background of her life. Now that he'd gone, there was a definite gap, and Alaska did seem very far away.

She also found it disturbing that he hadn't made much effort to say goodbye to her, despite his assurances that he was determined to remain in her life, and she could not get rid of him so easily. This new, exciting job had very soon tempted him away.

Again Judy's fingers stroked her cheek, and she pulled her hair forward over her face. She had been beginning to accept her changed looks but Blair's letter had shaken her confidence a little.

Yet surely this was what she had wanted, she reminded herself. She had told him he must go and leave her alone to come to terms with herself in her own way. Now he had done just that, she felt lonely and miserable.

For once she thought she'd like to talk to Alison about it, and she turned to watch the other girl as she sorted out her letters into bills and circulars, with a few personal letters to answer.

She hadn't noticed Judy's preoccupation, and now Judy longed to say something about Blair's letter but didn't know where to begin.

Judy watched Alison as she whisked her way into the bathroom, and the deep sense of loneliness she sometimes experienced beset her once more so that tears were not far away. She should be glad that Blair had gone away, but she hardly knew how she felt.

Slowly she began to wash up, her

mind on the rest of the household chores. House-keeping for Alison had been a great help, as she had spent little time on such mundane things in the past.

She had always been involved in studying or, later, her absorbing job at the laboratory.

She had convinced Alison that she needed to do simple jobs to keep herself busy, but for the first time she became a little irked by cleaning up and polishing. When Alison stopped for a break, and remarked that she could do with going to see Ian Thomson again, Judy eagerly offered to go for her.

'I need white card this time, Judy,' she said. 'It might be a bit awkward to carry.'

'I don't mind,' Judy said. 'I'll be glad of the walk.'

Alison smiled, her eyes tender. She wondered if Judy realised what progress she was making. It seemed hardly any time since Judy had had to be persuaded to go over the doorstep.

Now Alison suspected that Judy was becoming bored with staying in the flat, and that was a good sign.

'I'll be glad if you'd go for me, Judy,' she said. 'This drawing is turning out to be tricky, and there's a great deal of detail about it. I need to concentrate, but it's coming alive for me. I — I get a sort of feeling when I know it's going to be all right.'

Judy looked at her friend appraisingly and thought again about Blair's letter. Both he and Alison seemed to be absorbed in their jobs. Would the time come when she felt she could go back again to her own job?

Yet every time she thought about the laboratory, a queer blankness seemed to come over her mind, so that she would thrust all thought of it away. She could only think about it with fear and pain.

'I'll get the card for you, Alison,' she said quietly, and swung on her coat, then pulled out her headscarf. For a long moment she hesitated, then slowly she tied it over her head, and pulled it forward again. She didn't feel at all comfortable without it!

★ ★ ★

Ian Thomson was so pleased to see Judy when she arrived that it warmed her heart when she saw how his face lit up.

'Talk of the devil!' he cried, then laughed so heartily that Judy had to join in. 'I should say 'angel' in your case, Judy!' he said. 'I was planning to come round to see you this evening.'

'That'd be nice,' Judy said, still smiling. 'Before I forget, I want white card for Alison, and she hopes you have plenty in stock because she's going to need lots more.'

'Right,' Ian said, taking the note from Judy. 'Has she still got her nose to the grindstone? It must be a help having you to look after her, Judy.'

'I wonder,' Judy said musingly. 'At one time, no doubt, she stopped for a short time to make a break, but now

191

she does tend to go hard at it. I wonder if that's a good thing, Ian. I really do get so worried about her.'

'I know what you mean.' He nodded. 'Try to get her to relax in the evenings. Anyway, it was you I wanted to see, Judy. Have you ever heard of Malcolm Neill, the painter?'

Slowly Judy shook her head.

'He was in here, once, when you walked in. He picked something up for you.'

'Your magazines which Alison asked me to return,' Judy said. 'I remember. Was that Malcolm Neill? I seem to remember that he — he stared at me a lot. I wondered if it was my face . . .'

'I do know what you mean, Judy,' said Iain. 'If Mr Neill was staring at you, it was with the eyes of an artist. He's asked me to get in touch with you to see if you'll agree to meet him.'

Ian shrugged.

'Beyond that, though, I've no idea just what it's about, but I know it won't be anything which is likely to upset you.

I've known Mr Neill ever since I started the business and he's a very fine man. That's why I agreed to ask you for him.'

For a long moment Judy made no reply. Thoughtfully she stroked her cheek, her mind going once again to the middle-aged man who had stared at her so strangely.

She had sensed his very keen interest in her at the time, but always she had to cope with a sense of reluctance to meet new people. He was hardly likely to say or do anything to hurt her, but she found it hard to put away her fears.

'It's up to you, Judy,' Ian said very gently. 'I can soon explain things if you'd rather not see him. I wouldn't want to cause you any distress.'

'Let me think about it, Ian,' Judy said, with a smile. 'I'd better go back now with Alison's card, but — but I'll ring you. Will that do?'

'That will do just fine,' Ian said heartily. He had cut the white card for Alison, and now he fastened it together so that it would be easy to carry.

'Tell Alison not to work too hard,' Ian said. 'She'll be all the better for getting her breath back now and again.'

'I'll tell her,' Judy replied. 'Thanks, Ian.'

But her thoughts returned to Malcolm Neill as soon as she left the shop. Why did he want to speak to her, she asked herself? He had never seen her before the accident and couldn't know about the change in her appearance.

★   ★   ★

She managed the journey back to the flat in no time at all, and found that Alison was still so deeply absorbed in her work that she hardly answered when Judy walked in.

'Don't you think you could stop for a moment?' Judy asked. She had decided to tell Alison what had happened about Mr Neill and ask her advice, but the other girl was working with deep concentration.

'In a minute,' Alison murmured absently.

Judy sighed and went into the kitchen to prepare lunch. The walk had cleared her head and for the first time she realised that she had walked home without putting on her head-scarf. It was still in the pocket of her coat.

She'd been so busy thinking of Malcolm Neill and also of Blair, who seemed so very far away, that she had not noticed her hair blowing in the cool breeze. It had brought some colour into her cheeks and, as she caught sight of herself in the kitchen mirror, she managed to look at her own reflection without cringing.

Even before she set the table, and called to Alison to come and eat, she had made up her mind, which was just as well since Alison seemed to want to rush her lunch, then return to the drawing board at once.

'I'm going to meet a man,' Judy announced clearly. 'Ian's arranging it.'

'What?' Alison asked. 'A man? What sort of man?'

'An artist. One of those peculiar people who paint for a living!'

Alison grinned and aimed a bread pellet at her friend.

'Sorry, Judy,' she said, 'but my present drawing is going to come right, if I work at it. I just know it. But I've really got to work, you know.'

'I know,' Judy said. 'Do you want to hear about my artist, or not?'

'Of course I want to hear. What about him?'

'I saw him once at Ian's when I went to pick up some paints for you. He was already there, talking to Ian and . . . '

Judy paused, her brows wrinkling.

'He stared at me, Alison, but not in the usual way. He wasn't sorry for me, or anything like that. Now he wants to meet me, and he's asked Ian to arrange it. Ian says it's entirely up to me, but I think I might find it interesting to meet him.

'What's his name?' Alison asked.

'Malcolm Neill.'

'Malcolm Neill!' Alison's eyes were suddenly wide with interest. 'But he's a very well-known artist, Judy, and very successful. I should certainly want to meet him, if I . . . '

' . . . were you!' Judy finished, laughing as they both spoke the words together. 'It's all right, I've already made up my mind. I've got to telephone Ian with my decision.'

'Oh — telephone . . . ' Alison said, with her hand to her mouth. 'I forgot, Judy, but — but your mother was on the line, just to ask how we were. I had a nice little chat with her.'

'Oh,' Judy said non-committally.

'It's only natural, Judy,' Alison went on gently. 'She must get anxious at times, you know.'

'I know,' Judy said, sighing. 'I — I'll write to her, Alison. No need to go on about it.'

She could sense that Alison was waiting to hear more, but there were certain things in her mind which she didn't want to think about just yet. Her work was one thing and her relationship with her mother was another.

Not even Alison could be allowed a glimpse into her heart over these matters until she herself could come to terms with them. And now she was facing a third problem — that of Blair Walker having gone so far away, out of her life. That was leaving her with a very hollow, empty feeling.

Perhaps, by meeting Mr Neill and finding out what he had to say, she might also find something new to interest her.

'Well, back to work,' Alison said.

'Aren't you going to help wash up?' Judy asked sharply, and Alison paused, slightly taken aback. Was she beginning to take Judy for granted?

'Of course,' she agreed readily. 'I'm sorry, Judy. I didn't realise . . . '

'Oh, it's all right, Alison, I'll do it,' Judy told her. 'I'm just in a mood.'

Alison stood hesitating for a moment.

'Well, I'll make the tea,' she offered.

'Good. I'll hold you to that.'

But as Judy tidied up a little, she paused, quietly, to watch Alison's absorption in her work, and her own attention was immediately caught.

She was no art critic, but she could surely recognise quality when she saw it, and the standard of Alison's work was very high. Perhaps it's even outstanding, Judy thought. She had often admired the drawings and paintings which Alison had done, but this work was extraordinary.

Slowly she tiptoed away again and resolved to leave Alison alone, deciding such dedicated work should be encouraged. But when Alison eventually laid aside her brushes that evening, she looked very tired and Judy wondered if she had made a wise decision in not insisting that Alison should stop occasionally.

'Come on, Alison,' Judy said with determination. 'Put on your flatties and let's go for a walk round the park.'

'Oh dear, I don't really feel like it,'

Alison responded. 'I just want to watch something on TV.'

'You used to make me walk,' Judy reminded her. 'Come on, now it's my turn. You'll feel better for it.'

'Tomorrow,' Alison said.

'Mañana.' Judy sighed. 'All right then, tomorrow. How on earth did Alec put up with you?'

Alison's eyes darkened and Judy felt she could have bitten her tongue.

'I'm sorry, Alison,' she said huskily. 'Let's just watch TV.'

The following afternoon, when Alison was busily working once again, Judy decided she needed a break even if Alison didn't.

'I think I'll call round at Ian's instead of phoning, Alison,' she called. 'I feel like a walk and I'll tell him I've decided to meet Mr Neill. I'll pick up your paint-brushes while I'm there.'

'OK then,' Alison called back.

Judy wondered if she'd really taken in what she'd said, and shrugged her shoulders as she went out the door. She was worried about Alison. Being so involved in one thing couldn't be healthy.

* * *

Alison glanced at the time much later in the afternoon and wished that Judy had not forgotten her key as the doorbell shrilled, then shrilled again. She laid aside her finest brush, and wiped her sticky fingers before going to the door.

'Back at last,' she cried, as she threw it open. 'Oh . . . '

She was startled for a moment when she saw a tall, slender girl standing outside. 'I — I'm sorry,' she said. 'I thought you were someone else. Can I help you?'

'Yes, please. Can you tell me if Dr Judy Millar is staying here?'

Alison's eyes narrowed a little.

'Yes, she is staying here . . . '

'Oh, I'm so glad,' the girl said. 'I rang up her home and I was given this address. I expect you're Mrs Drummond. I'm Sue Reynolds. I — I work with Dr Millar. I wonder if I could see her, please?'

Alison hesitated for another moment, then she stood back.

'Please come in,' she said quietly. 'I'm afraid Dr Millar is out at the moment, but if you're a colleague . . . '

'I'm not exactly a colleague,' the girl said rather awkwardly. 'As a matter of fact. I was Dr Millar's assistant when that awful accident happened. She saved me when I made a terrible mistake. It — it's all my fault that she got so badly injured.'

Alison had invited the girl to sit down, and now she sat down herself as she stared at Sue Reynolds. She could hardly believe that the girl who had been the cause of so much distress to Judy, however unwittingly, was now sitting by her fireside.

'You must forgive me, but I feel rather taken aback,' she said with difficulty. 'You seem to have arrived out of the blue. May I ask what you're doing here?'

Suddenly Alison could see the nervous twitching of the girl's fingers as they looked at one another.

'I had to come,' Sue said huskily. 'I've been thinking about Dr Millar for weeks, only — it just gets worse and worse. I just — I *must* see her. I must know how she's coping, but nobody seems able to tell me.

'I've got three days' leave, so I booked in at a hotel in Edinburgh and then I came along here straightaway.'

Alison tried to hang on to her scattered wits and looked again at the time. Judy was making such good progress, but what would happen if she walked in and found Sue Reynolds here? How would she take it if she suddenly came face to face with the girl who had caused the accident?

Rather wildly Alison decided that she must insist on the girl leaving immediately. Judy might wish to see her, but she must be prepared first of all.

'Look, Sue,' she said urgently, 'I can assure you that Dr Millar is making good progress, but I hope you'll understand if I prefer that you don't see her just yet. I'll certainly tell her you've called and if you let me know where you're staying, I'll get in touch.'

'Are you sure she is getting better?' Sue asked, her eyes full of anxiety as she named the hotel. 'I really do want to see her.'

'And so you will, I'm sure, but not suddenly — like this . . . '

A moment later there was the sound of footsteps, and the door was flung open.

'Alison!' Judy cried rather breathlessly. 'Guess where I'm going tomorrow . . . Oh! Oh, it's you . . . '

Sue Reynolds rose slowly to her feet, her eyes glued to Judy's face.

Who Could She Turn To?

WHY, Sue!' Judy exclaimed. 'Sue Reynolds! What on earth are you doing here?'

Judy had been smiling as she walked into the room, but now time seemed to stand still as the younger girl rose to her feet, her eyes full of horror and distress.

Judy's eyes darkened when she saw Sue's expression and she quickly turned away, murmuring that she must remove her coat and scarf. Even as she put her coat on a hanger, Judy was collecting her thoughts.

Sue's reaction had stabbed like a knife, but she knew it was inevitable after what had caused the accident, and Sue was too young to hide her feelings. But Judy was learning how to cope with such a situation, and as she turned back to the other two girls she was quite composed again.

She had caught the look of anxiety in Alison's face and she smiled at her reassuringly.

'I felt I had to come, Doctor Millar,' Sue was saying. 'No-one could tell me anything about you and I felt I just had to come.'

'Well, as you'll have noticed, I'm quite fit again, Sue,' Judy said quietly, as she sat down by the fireside. Sue had also sat down again, though Alison could see her face was very white and she was obviously shaken.

'It's my turn to make the tea,' she said brightly. 'We take turns, you know — Judy and I. You'll join us, of course, Sue?'

'I'd love a cup of tea,' the girl murmured. 'It's sometimes difficult to get a cup of tea at a hotel.'

'You're staying in Edinburgh then?' Judy asked as she turned again to Sue after Alison had gone into the kitchen. 'Are you on holiday?'

'I — no, I'm not on holiday,' she confessed. 'As a matter of fact, I've resigned, Doctor Millar. I just couldn't carry on, not after the accident.'

There was a short silence, then Sue continued with a rush. 'It was on my conscience, you see, I couldn't concentrate any more. I knew it was all my fault. Goodness knows you warned me often enough.'

Gradually, Judy was beginning to see that she had not been the only victim of the accident. Sue Reynolds had also suffered, even if it had been deep inside herself.

Alison had appeared with the tea tray, and Judy stood up to help her friend to set it out, and to pour out tea.

'No sugar for Sue,' Judy said, smiling at her former colleague and, for the first time, there was a rush of tears to the girl's eyes.

'Fancy you remembering that,' she said shakily.

'Oh, there's quite a lot I remember!' Judy said, turning to Alison. 'This young lady has given up her job, Alison. I must say I'm disappointed to hear that. It isn't the sort of job that can be done by everyone, and Sue was gaining experience . . . '

'And making mistakes,' Sue said quietly.

'We learn by our mistakes,' Judy replied gently. 'And the bigger the mistake, the better the lesson. You must try to get another job in the same field, Sue.'

'But meantime I hope she'll turn this trip into a proper holiday,' Alison put in, 'and see a bit of Edinburgh while she's here. The hotel isn't far away, Sue, so feel free to call in here, at the flat, whenever you want to.'

The other girl smiled shyly, then glanced at Judy as if for approval.

'Alison's right, you mustn't make yourself a stranger,' Judy said, 'especially since I want to hear all about what's been going on since I've been away from the lab. How is Dr Rutherford? We hear from him now and again, but . . . '

'Oh, he's as busy as ever,' Sue said. 'I

used to find him a bit scary, but he's been very kind and understanding. He's not nearly as frightening as you'd think.'

Alison hid a smile as she remembered how easy everything had been in Charles Rutherford's company. Yet she could imagine that some of the younger employees might regard him with great respect and a little bit of awe.

'He must have a lot to do,' Judy was saying thoughtfully.

'He's got a temporary assistant,' Sue said. 'Dr Mason — Adele Mason. She's a tall girl with dark hair.'

'I know Dr Mason.' Judy nodded. 'She's very beautiful.' Again there was silence.

'What else has happened?' Sue said, voicing her thoughts. 'Oh, yes, Stephen Hunter, one of the lab technicians, got married and we had a whip round for a present. And Jimmy Martin took another course at the polytechnic and passed with distinction.'

'Good for Jimmy!' Judy said warmly.

'I must send Stephen a gift. Do we know his bride?'

Sue shook her head.

'No. He met her on holiday. Sometimes holiday romances work out, it seems.'

★ ★ ★

Alison had just cleared away the cups when the doorbell rang again.

'My, we're popular today,' she said, as she opened the door to find Ian Thomson standing on the step.

'Hello, Alison,' he greeted her, smiling. 'Is Judy home? Oh . . . '

He paused when he saw that there was a third girl present, and Alison made the introductions.

'Is everything all right, Judy?' he asked her, and she nodded.

'Everything's fine, Ian,' she reassured him, and saw him relax with relief.

'In that case, you shouldn't have walked out without Alison's new paint brushes.' He grinned and produced a small parcel from his overcoat pocket.

'Oh dear. I'm sorry,' Judy said. 'My head's like a sieve!'

'You're forgiven,' Ian said, while Alison thanked him for his trouble.

Sue Reynolds had picked up her handbag, and a guide book and map of Edinburgh which Alison had lent her.

'I'll really have to go now,' she said. 'I've got to get back to the hotel. I'll be quite lost if it gets too dark.'

'Which hotel?' Ian asked. 'Perhaps I could take you there.'

'Oh, would you, Ian?' Judy asked. 'It would save us worrying about Sue.'

She turned to Sue. 'Alison and I will both be busy tomorrow, but if you can manage to come along in the evening we'll be very pleased to see you. I'll probably think of a hundred questions I want to ask after you've gone.'

'I'll be glad to do that,' Sue said, and Alison looked on with interest.

She could see that Sue still stared at Judy very anxiously when she thought Judy wasn't looking. The girl could do with a holiday, Alison thought, oblivious to her own fatigue, though she knew that this time off might mean she would have to work later this evening.

After the door closed behind Ian and Sue, Judy again dropped into her armchair rather wearily.

'Sue's had an upsetting time, too, Judy,' Alison said, coming to sit beside her. 'I suppose you'll find it difficult not to — to blame her a little.'

Judy shook her head. 'It was an accident, and it's over now. I've got to put it behind me, Alison, and frankly, so has Sue.'

'Yes, you're right,' Alison replied. 'So when are you seeing Malcolm Neill?'

'He wants me to go to his studio tomorrow afternoon. From what Ian says I think he must want me to look at one of his paintings. I wouldn't go, Alison, except that Ian can vouch for him and says he's a very fine man. Also — why, I don't know — but he sounds as though he's someone I could like and trust. Besides . . .'

'Come off it, you're just as curious as Ian!' Alison finished, and both girls laughed heartily.

'You could say that,' Judy admitted.

For a while they spoke about things in general, then Alison rose wearily to her feet.

'Will you be all right just watching TV, Judy?' she asked.

'Why? Are you going out?'

'Going out! No such luck,' Alison said. 'I have some work to finish.'

'But you can't work this late, Alison.' Judy protested. 'It would be pointless. You'd just have to scrap it in the morning.'

'Oh, not nowadays,' Alison said. 'I've got so used to working into the wee, small hours. I really must finish these paintings I'm doing. I have other work waiting now, Judy, and it's got to be done. If I don't turn it in, the publishers might think I'm too slow, and the commission will go to someone else.'

'I don't see that a few hours will

make any difference,' Judy said dubiously.

Alison's hands were beginning to shake a little and Judy noticed it when Alison had poured the tea for Sue Reynolds. She really was working too hard.

'I must keep to my schedule,' Alison was saying firmly, and Judy could find no further argument.

The following afternoon Judy dressed carefully for her visit to Malcolm Neill's studio.

Alison had suggested that she should take a taxi, but after a bit of thought Judy had decided to go by bus part of the way, and walk the rest. She was getting used to going out in public again.

In fact, Judy's thoughts were more on Alison than Malcolm Neill. It had been very late when she had finished work the previous evening, yet when Judy rose in the morning, Alison was up before her and was once again at her drawing board.

Judy had made no protest but when she brewed up coffee for breakfast she had quietly walked over to the corner of the room known as Alison's 'studio' and handed her a cup of steaming hot coffee.

A new project was taking shape under her skilful fingers and the work she had just completed had been spread out on a table to dry.

Judy studied it in earnest and once again the sheer brilliance of Alison's paintings struck her. No-one could doubt that she had a masterly touch, but the price she had paid for this quality was there to be seen in her frail, trembling fingers and white, strained face.

Judy wanted to pull her away from the drawing board and force her to take a long rest, well away from all thoughts of art, but she knew she would gain nothing unless Alison herself was willing to co-operate.

Judy pursed her lips, wondering where she could turn for help, and Ken

Doig was the first person to spring to mind — perhaps he could give her some advice.

She'd make some excuse to Alison for leaving early to keep her appointment with Mr Neill, and call in to have a word with Ken on the way.

In the end Alison was too absorbed to notice the time, and Judy quietly left the flat and turned to walk briskly towards Ken's shop.

She had bought herself a new dress, with a matching hat which had a pulldown brim, and she had put away the headscarf which she was beginning to hate.

Ken's pleasure in Judy's improved appearance made her visit to the shop seem worthwhile on her own account as well as Alison's.

'Judy, how nice to see you!' he exclaimed. 'Do you have time for a cup of tea in the office?'

'No tea, thanks, Ken,' she said. 'I've got an appointment at three. I — I just wanted to buy some refills for my ball-point pen and . . . ' She hesitated, then said, 'Oh, all right, Ken, perhaps a cup of tea would be nice.'

'Are you watching your figure, or can I offer you a biscuit?' Ken asked, grinning, after his secretary had brought them a tray. 'It's a chocolate one.'

'Go on then, you've twisted my arm.' Judy laughed.

'And how's Alison?' he asked, coming to put her tea down on a small table.

Judy's smile faded, and her eyes were grave as they met his.

'Oh, Ken, I don't know what to say, except that I've been getting more and more worried about her over the past few days.'

'Why?' Ken's voice was sharp.

'She's working far too hard. No, it's more than that. Her work's becoming an obsession with her, Ken. At first she just seemed to stick at it in a sort of dedicated way, but gradually she started doing extra bits at night.'

Judy sighed deeply.

'Now she's working at night as a matter of course, and she hardly takes time off to eat. I don't even know if she's sleeping properly, because she's out of bed early in the morning and back at the drawing board before I'm even up! And her hand has started to shake. I'm sure that's a sign of strain, Ken.'

'I — I see.' His brown eyes grew solemn.

'Maybe I shouldn't be running to you with our worries, Ken.'

'Don't be daft!' he said sharply. 'Who else should you turn to? I'm glad you came to tell me. You must know I'm very fond of Alison.'

'I know,' She smiled gently.

'Don't go worrying yourself too much, Judy,' he told her. 'I'll certainly do what I can to help. We can't have her making herself ill with overwork.'

He paused, his expression puzzled.

'Anyway, surely she doesn't need to work so hard for — for financial reasons . . . ?'

Once again his eyes darkened when he remembered that Alison had insisted on paying back the money Alec had borrowed. Surely that wasn't the reason for all this overwork?

'No, it isn't the money, Ken,' Judy was saying. 'I'm afraid it goes deeper than that. It's like a compulsion.' She put down her cup then glanced at her watch. 'Good grief, I'll have to go, Ken, but I'm glad I've told you.'

Ken nodded and escorted Judy through the shop. Alison might not thank him for interfering in her life but it had to be done. And there was no-one to do it but himself.

* * *

Judy caught a bus outside Ken's shop, and a short time later she was walking towards Malcolm Neill's studio.

It was on the ground floor of a fine Georgian building and when she rang the bell the door was opened so promptly she felt Mr Neill must have been watching for her.

His face lit up in a smile of welcome when he saw her on the step.

'Miss Millar — Doctor Millar,' he amended. 'I'm so glad you came.'

Judy looked round curiously as Mr Neill took her coat and hat, then led the way into a long, airy room filled with light from huge windows which had taken the place of an outside wall.

'My word, what a bright room!' she said appreciatively. 'Alison would love this.'

'Alison?'

'My friend, Alison Drummond. She's an artist, too, though I think you'd call her a commercial artist. She does wonderful work, though. She's sold her illustrations to lots of book publishers and has done quite a bit of magazine work.'

Judy bit her lip, aware that her nervousness was making her talk too much, but Mr Neill seemed to be very interested.

'I'd very much like to meet her some

time,' he said, 'and to see her work.'

Judy turned her attention to the various pictures hanging round the studio and to the canvases stacked against the walls.

However, before she could examine them more closely, Mr Neill had taken her arm and led her towards a tall easel which stood in a corner.

Quickly he took the cover off the easel and turned it towards Judy. It was the portrait of a young woman, and Judy gasped with amazement as she looked at it.

It was a portrait of — of herself!

She looked at the face which was now becoming so familiar to her and which she had come to accept as her own. Yet there was something not quite right. It wasn't an exact likeness . . .

Mr Neill was watching her with a smile on his face.

'Well?' he asked gently. 'Do you see the likeness, Doctor Millar?'

The likeness? Judy looked at the portrait again.

'Who is it?' she asked quietly.

'My late wife, Lorna,' Mr Neill replied. 'The portrait isn't finished, as you see. I — I simply never got round to it. I left it like this for more years than I care to remember, then I lost her before I could finish it. Lorna needed an operation, you see, and she didn't recover.'

'Oh, I'm so sorry,' Judy said with genuine sympathy.

'Well, it was some years ago now,' Mr Neill continued, 'but I'm sure you can understand my interest when I met you, Doctor Millar. You're so very, very like her.'

He was walking about, looking at her from all angles, but for once Judy didn't mind such close scrutiny.

'I couldn't explain properly to Ian,' he told her. 'I could only show you the portrait, and hope you'd appreciate my great interest in your appearance.'

'Oh, I do,' Judy agreed. 'At first I actually thought the portrait was of myself.'

'There are a few small differences,' Mr Neill said, and Judy could see the artist in him taking over as he outlined the broad, sweet forehead, and the curve of the cheek.

'You have more width here, and Lorna's jawline was a little more prominent, but your eyes are very much alike. I'm sure you take a keen interest in all you do, Doctor Millar, just as Lorna did.'

He smiled, remembering.

'It comes over in the expression of the eyes, and the set of the mouth. And the nose is perfect, quite perfect . . . ' he repeated, his voice tailing off as he gazed again at the portrait.

'I couldn't finish the hair. As you see, I sketched it in lightly and laid on the basic colour, but the highlights are missing. She had beautiful hair, just like you, only she wore it in a rather different style . . . '

Again his voice tailed off and there was a long silence while Mr Neill seemed to lose himself in the portrait.

⋆　⋆　⋆

'Er, would you like me to sit for you so that you can finish the portrait? Is that it?' Judy asked the artist rather nervously.

Gradually the reason why Mr Neill had taken such an interest in her appearance was becoming clear to her. She had sensed that his absorption was unusual, and now it was easy to see why.

Now he seemed to pull himself together.

'What? Sit for me in order to finish the portrait? Oh, dear me, no. Though you look very like Lorna, no two people are so alike that one can take the place of another.'

Then his expression brightened.

'But I would like you to sit for a portrait of yourself. I'm sure I don't have to explain the pleasure that would give me.'

They regarded one another silently for a long moment, then Judy nodded.

'I can see it would give you some professional pleasure, Mr Neill,' she said quietly, 'but — but I'd like to think it over, if you don't mind. I'd like to tell Alison, my friend, and see what she thinks.'

'Of course you must think about it. I wouldn't like you to agree to this lightly. It may mean a few sittings and that wouldn't be very easy for you. Just ask any professional model! Besides, you may feel reluctant to spare the time.'

'Oh, I've got plenty of time, Mr Neill,' Judy said quietly.

She took another long look at the portrait, then Mr Neill began to show her round his studio.

With each new picture she looked at, her admiration for Malcolm Neill's talent grew, and she could see why he had built up such a high reputation.

'They're beautiful,' she said softly. 'Thank you for showing me your pictures, Mr Neill.'

He smiled and nodded acceptance of

her compliments.

'Will you telephone when you've decided what you want to do?' Mr Neill asked.

'Yes, I won't keep you waiting,' Judy promised. 'I'll telephone you either way very soon, Mr Neill.'

Judy left the studio and felt she could hardly wait to get home to see Alison. But if she was going to be out most of the day sitting for Mr Neill, would that be a good thing for her friend?

Would it force her to stop work and cook meals for herself, or would it be even worse for her if she forgot to stop for a break at all?

Judy thought about Ken Doig and wondered if he could reason with Alison.

After Judy had left, Ken had become involved in a long telephone conversation with an important customer but, as soon as he hung up the receiver, he reached for his coat. Quickly he leafed over the papers on his desk and gave his secretary some instructions before he hurried away.

'I may be a little while, Anna,' he said, handing her a scribbled note. 'You can reach me at this number if you need me.'

'OK, Mr Doig,' Anna said with a brisk nod.

On his way to the flat, Ken's thoughts were all on Alison. He had seen her a few days ago and had thought she looked rather pale and tired.

As he bounded up the stairs to the flat, he could see a young girl, tall and slender, with long dark hair, standing outside the door. She turned to stare at him anxiously as he came towards her.

'Hello,' Ken said. 'Are you calling on Mrs Drummond?'

'I'm a — a friend of Dr Millar's,' she told him. 'I'm Sue Reynolds. I used to work with her.'

'And I was at school with both Alison and Judy,' Ken laughed, as he introduced himself. 'Alison's taking her time.'

He rang the bell again. 'I wonder if she's gone out.'

'She said she'd be in.' Sue said rather anxiously. 'She's expecting me at this time. I phoned earlier. Dr Millar is out, but Mrs Drummond was working.'

Ken's eyes were worried as they met Sue's. Swiftly he turned the door handle. It stuck a little but Ken applied a little pressure and the door flew open.

Even as he and Sue stepped into the flat, they could hear the sound of someone moaning.

'Think About It'

Sue Reynolds' eyes widened with shock when she heard the low moaning sound.

'It's Alison!' she cried, but already Ken was striding through to the kitchen, where Alison had fallen just behind the door. He knelt down beside her then looked at Sue as she immediately came over to see what had happened.

'I'll lift her through to the settee,' he said, after he had quickly made sure that she was not badly injured. 'She seems to have hurt her knee.'

His face was very white and Sue could see how concerned he was for the girl who now lay unconscious on the floor. Without a word, Sue held open the doors so Ken could lift Alison through to the settee, where the other girl piled up cushions beneath her head.

'She's as light as a feather,' Ken whispered with concern. 'I'd noticed she'd lost a great deal of weight recently, but I didn't realise how frail she had become until now.'

'Can't we get her to bed?' Sue asked. 'I'll undress her, and perhaps you could ring for the doctor.'

It had been a shock for Ken to see Alison lying unconscious like that. It took him a moment or two to pull himself together and think what they should do.

'Yes, she'll be more comfortable in bed. I can manage to carry her through quite easily. Apart from her knee, I can't see any signs of injury, though she'll be carrying some nasty bruises around for a week or two. She certainly needs the doctor, though.'

Sue nodded, and a moment later she was shutting the bedroom door before turning to make Alison comfortable in bed. The older girl moaned again, and opened her eyes so that Sue put a hand on her soothingly.

'Oh dear,' Alison whispered. 'What . . . ? I fell . . . I don't feel very well . . .'

Sue reassured Alison that she and Ken would look after her, then made her as comfortable as she could. Her words to Alison had sounded confident, but watching the pale, ill-looking figure lying on the bed, she couldn't help but be concerned.

Sue was smoothing the fair hair from Alison's forehead, when Ken tapped lightly on the bedroom door. She opened it and he walked over to look down on Alison.

'She came round for a moment,' Sue said, 'but she appears to be exhausted. She has no strength in her at all.'

'The doctor will be here shortly,' Ken said. 'He looked after Alison when — when Alec was killed.'

'Alec?' The girl looked puzzled.

'Her husband,' Ken explained. 'He was going into business with me, but he was killed in a car accident.'

'Oh, how terrible,' Sue said with sympathy. 'My own troubles seem so trivial in comparison.'

'I know what you mean,' Ken agreed. His eyes rested gently on Sue for a moment. The girl looked far too young to be worried by trouble of any kind, he thought.

Alison began to stir again and this time it was Ken who took her hand. A moment later the bell shrilled and Dr Frazer was shown in by Sue.

For Ken the minutes seemed to drag past while the doctor examined Alison. Finally he came through to join Ken and Sue in the sitting-room.

'Well, she'll be fine after a rest — but I do mean a rest,' the doctor said rather heavily. 'That young woman is a prime example of working oneself to a standstill. Her knee will be painful for a day or two but I don't think it will trouble her for long.

'However, I must stress that she is not to sit at that drawing-board until I give her the all clear.' Dr Frazer stated firmly. 'She's strained herself to the limit and I've just told her so.'

The tablets which the doctor had given Alison had taken effect and, when Sue and Ken went to look at her, she was sleeping deeply. By this time Sue felt in need of a rest herself, but a moment later they heard Judy's key in the lock, and they both hurried to the door to meet her.

Judy was looking brighter and more animated than Ken had seen her for some time, though her eyes grew alarmed when she saw Ken and Sue waiting for her.

'Hello, Ken — and Sue ... What's the matter? Where's Alison?'

'In bed,' Ken said briefly. 'Now, don't get alarmed. She collapsed in the kitchen and she's hurt her knee a little, but she's asleep now. Sue and I got her to bed and the doctor has just called.'

'Oh, no.' She gasped.

'There isn't too much wrong, Judy,' Ken said gently. 'It's just what you suspected — she's been doing too much. The doctor says that after a few days' rest she'll be fine.'

Judy hurried through to look at Alison, then returned to the sitting-room a few minutes later.

'Maybe her injured knee is a blessing in disguise,' she said. 'She'll have to rest now. Thanks for all you've done — both of you. What a good job you were here! Alison might have lain till I arrived home.'

'She'd probably have come round and put herself to bed.' Ken said reassuringly. 'There's no thanks necessary.' He turned to help Sue with her coat. 'I'll be round again tomorrow to see how she's getting on. I'll see you then, Judy.'

'OK — thanks . . . ' Judy said rather absently.

She was feeling rather shocked by what had happened and was glad to sit down and get her breath back.

*   *   *

As Ken and Sue walked downstairs together, he turned to smile at her.

'I don't know about you, Sue, but now that Alison's comfortable and being looked after, I find myself with a healthy appetite. What about you?'

'Well — I only had a sandwich at lunchtime,' the girl replied, with a smile.

'Then I think we ought to have a decent dinner,' Ken declared. 'There's a hotel just farther along here to the right which serves a good meal. We'll go in there.'

The hotel was warm and comfortable, and Sue looked round appreciatively. She was going to enjoy her holiday in Edinburgh, she decided, now that she was getting used to Dr Millar's changed appearance.

Her eyes had grown solemn as she thought about Judy and the reason for her own visit to Edinburgh, so that she started, then blushed a little, when Ken offered her a penny for her thoughts.

'I — I was just thinking about Dr Millar,' she confessed. 'I don't suppose you know it, but I was responsible for her accident.'

Ken's eyebrows rose and he could see the distress in the girl's eyes.

'You say 'accident,'' he repeated, 'and I've always understood it was just that.'

'In a way, but it *was* due to my carelessness.' Sue said, lowering her head.

Ken was silent for a moment. 'Are you sure it was carelessness? Or was it not, perhaps, just lack of experience? I know nothing about Judy's job, but I believe it's very exacting.'

'Oh, it is,' Sue agreed. 'She'd warned me several times, but I forgot for a moment and then it was too late. Dr Millar pushed me out of the way, and — and she was injured.'

'I see.' Ken said. 'And now you find that hard to live with?'

Sue nodded. 'I gave up my job, and I've come to Edinburgh to see her. I — I just couldn't settle.'

'No, I know the feeling,' Ken agreed. 'I sent Alec Drummond away on an errand in my car and he had the accident in which he died. I often ask myself if I did the right thing.'

They were silent for a moment, as the waiter served up their order.

'So often we have to learn to live with ourselves,' Ken murmured. 'But I'm quite sure Judy doesn't blame you.'

'No, she's been marvellous.' Sue smiled. Her appetite had dwindled for a moment, but now it returned and she tackled her steak with enjoyment. It helped to know she wasn't the only one with such a weight of guilt.

'At least I'll see a bit of Edinburgh while I'm here,' she went on. 'Alison lent me some maps but I've bought one of my own and I was returning hers when you met me at the top of the stairs.'

'It can be tiring if you don't know your way about,' Ken commented. 'I'll tell you what, sometimes I have to deliver goods in my car, so I could pick you up now and again and take you to some of the interesting places. I'll just take a note of your hotel and the telephone number.'

'Oh, that would be kind!' Sue exclaimed happily.

★ ★ ★

Alison felt much better by the time Dr Frazer called again, though she leaned back tiredly on her pillows while the doctor gave Judy firm instructions for building up Alison's strength.

'I'll do everything necessary for a day or two,' Judy said, after he had gone.

'The first thing to do is to ring up my publishers, if you don't mind,' Alison said ruefully. 'I can't start on that new project this week.'

'Or next!' Judy stated firmly.

'They'll have to know.' Alison nodded. 'And can you answer the other letters, too, please, Judy? I'll have to turn down those offers of work. By the way, what happened when you went to see Malcolm Neill?'

Judy's eyes gleamed again.

'He wants to paint my portrait, Alison. It was the most extraordinary thing. He showed me a portrait of his late wife and, well, quite honestly, Alison, it could have been me, as I am now!'

'How strange.' Alison said, her interest immediately caught. 'When do you start to sit for him?'

'Well . . . ' Judy paused awkwardly. Now that Alison had taken ill, it was not going to be so easy to leave her.

'When?' Alison repeated, reading her mind.

'Friday afternoon, two-thirty,' Judy answered reluctantly.

'Well, you be there at two-twenty-nine,' Alison said sternly. 'And don't worry about me. I'll obey Dr Frazer's instructions. Oh dear, I do feel sleepy all of a sudden.'

Her eyelids were growing heavy.

'I hope the publishers can wait for a week or two, though,' she mumbled. 'I won't go so hard at it and tire myself out again, if only they'll wait.'

The next few days until Friday passed slowly for Judy, though she was kept busy at the flat. Sue Reynolds called quite often and was a great help with running errands, and Ken turned up with a huge bunch of flowers for the invalid.

'Gracious — were there any left in the flower shop?' Alison asked, with a giggle.

'I'm going back for the rest tomorrow,' Ken promised. 'It's just so good to see you sitting up and taking notice again. I'd much rather talk to you than to an animated paintbrush!'

'Oh, Ken!' Alison laughed. 'I haven't thanked you yet for all you did for me — you and Sue. Poor Sue! What a way to spend her holiday.'

'She didn't mind at all,' Ken said warmly. 'She's a very nice girl. I took her to the Palace of Holyrood House yesterday afternoon and she appreciated it so much that I must say I began to see it for myself — really see it, I mean — all over again.'

'Yes, I know what you mean, Ken,' Alison agreed.

She had been allowed out of bed and was now resting on a large old chesterfield, with a warm woollen rug over her knees.

Judy and Sue had taken the massive bunch of flowers into the kitchen and were arranging them in various containers.

When the bell rang and Ian Thomson came in with another offering of flowers, there was a great deal of happy laughter whilst the girls hurriedly searched for a few extra vases.

'I don't care if we have flowers on every inch of space,' said Alison. 'They're beautiful, and I can only thank you both very much.'

'When are you due to go back home, Sue?' Ian asked, after he and Ken acknowledged Alison's thanks.

'I'd planned to return home on Saturday but I've decided to stay for an extra week,' Sue said, smiling. 'I — I've rather fallen in love with Edinburgh.'

Alison lay back on the settee, smiling at her friends, though her eyes were thoughtful when she saw the way Sue's face had lit up when she described her visit to the Castle, and how much more interesting it had been with Ken as a guide.

She looked from one to the other, and her heart lurched a little so that once again she experienced a twinge of loneliness.

Over the past few months she had been taking Ken's support and his friendship very much for granted but, for the first time, she realised it might not always be so readily available. There was bound to come a time when someone else would be more important to him than she was.

Feeling suddenly depressed, Alison closed her eyes and leaned back against the cushions so that Judy called a halt to the light-hearted banter.

'Alison's tired,' she said. 'I think she should rest now.'

'I'm already on my way,' Ian joked.

'My queue of customers will be meeting me along the street.'

'I must go, too,' Ken said. 'Can I drop you anywhere, Sue?'

'Oh yes, please,' she said. 'I'd like to go to the nearest post office.'

'I'll see you on Saturday then, Alison,' Ken said. 'You really must continue to rest, you know.'

Alison nodded, but her smile wavered after they had gone. She had very little choice at the moment.

*   *   *

On Friday Judy left for her appointment with Malcolm Neill a few minutes late, having spent the morning fussing round Alison.

'I've changed your library book,' she said, 'and here are some magazines. A flask of coffee and biscuits, tissues on the table, the radio ... Is that everything?'

'Oh, Judy!' Alison laughed. 'Please don't think up anything else. Really, I'll be perfectly all right with all these things. My knee is a lot better, and I can walk, you know.'

'Not yet,' Judy pleaded. 'Just another two days, until Dr Frazer sees you again, then you can begin to go out a little, but I don't want you to have another giddy spell.'

'OK, I promise.' Alison said. 'You know, you look really nice in that outfit.'

'Yes, it is quite smart,' Judy agreed, her cheeks a little flushed.

It seemed strange that she could take an interest in clothes again, but having her portrait painted had made her conscious of her appearance in a different sort of way. Now she was anxious to make the best of herself instead of trying to hide her face.

Nevertheless, as she glanced at her watch when she stepped off the bus near Malcolm Neill's studio. Judy realised that she would have to hurry, and she was a little out of breath when she rang the bell.

Once again the door was opened and Mr Neill welcomed her in with undisguised pleasure, and perhaps a little bit of relief, on his face.

'I'm sorry I'm late,' she said. 'My friend hasn't been well, and I wanted to make sure she'd everything she needed before I left.'

'No need to apologise,' Mr Neill replied. 'I'm just — just pleased you have come.'

How nice he was, Judy thought, and how welcome he made her feel. He had obviously made comprehensive preparations for starting work on the portrait, and he had placed a chair in front of a cream silken back-cloth.

'Just comb your hair through with your fingers — it's beautiful. That's it. Now, are you comfortable?'

'Quite comfortable, thank you.' She tried to compose herself.

'Can you hold that pose? You may talk if you wish, but I would like you to hold your head steady.'

'I'll do my best,' Judy said, smiling.

She was feeling a trifle self-conscious and for a few minutes her cheeks were pink again, but gradually Mr Neill's deep, rather soothing voice settled her nerves.

'I forgot to ask if it's inconvenient for you to sit for me on Fridays,' he said. 'I wondered, later, if it would interfere with your work?'

'I — I'm not working at the moment, Mr Neill,' Judy's voice faltered. 'I suppose you will have noticed that I've been in an accident.'

'Eh — what?' Mr Neill asked almost absently.

'I had an accident,' she repeated, and went on to tell him about it. Somehow it was easy to talk to Mr Neill about her face, since his whole concentration appeared to be centred on reproducing her features on to canvas.

'So you've been trying to hide yourself away,' he said gently, 'until you realised that the only one who really minded about those scars was yourself.'

She was silent for a moment.

'I think others did mind,' she said at length. 'My mother did . . . Or she did before I had the plastic surgery.'

She hadn't been able to speak about her mother up until now, thought Judy, with an ache in her heart. Now she found herself reliving those early days, and her own reaction to the horror on Mrs Millar's face.

'I know that I must have looked hideous,' she said.

'Perhaps you also knew that your mother's reaction was born out of her love for you and how *you* would feel about your own appearance,' Mr Neill said. 'I expect she would rejoice with you equally well when she saw how greatly the plastic surgery has helped.'

'I — I don't know,' Judy said, in a a low voice. It was a new thought to her that her mother would be upset because of how she, Judy, would feel about it. Judy had always thought that the reaction was for herself.

'Think about it,' Mr Neill said quietly, regarding her steadily. 'Perhaps that will do for today,' he said, changing the subject abruptly.

'I don't suppose I can see what you have done?' Judy asked.

'I've only just started,' Mr Neill replied, shaking his head. 'We'll need several sittings.'

He smiled and Judy found herself thinking how likeable he was, and how much better she felt for having talked to him. He had already given her one or two things to think about.

* * *

Judy walked to the bus stop with a light step. Somehow she felt that a friendship had been formed which could prove to be very precious to her.

She thought about her mother, and wondered whether Mr Neill was right. Perhaps her mother had been more shattered than anyone else she knew, simply because she loved Judy so much.

For the first time the girl put herself in her mother's place, and began to realise a little of what she had felt.

I'll ring her and have a friendly chat, Judy promised herself, and I'll see how things go.

The following morning Judy was up early. She and Alison had invited Sue Reynolds for lunch and Judy felt in the mood to cook something nice for all three of them.

Alison looked at Judy's bright face and decided that having one's portrait painted did a lot for a girl. Rather wryly she wondered if she ought to have tried that form of painting herself!

Judy had brought her a cup of tea in bed but Alison insisted that she was now quite well enough to get up. She found Judy reading the paper as she ate toast and marmalade at the kitchen table.

'Do you mind if I cut something out of the paper, Alison?' she asked. 'I don't know whether Sue would be interested, but there's a job here which would just suit her. She's obviously so happy to be here in Edinburgh that she might like to stay on for a few months.'

Alison passed over the scissors and picked up her own mail.

'I don't mind if you cut out the advert,' she said, though again she experienced the small stab of desolation. At least Ken might be pleased, she thought, if Sue stayed on. He seemed to enjoy her company very much.

There was a letter from her publishers and Alison opened it, her mind still on Sue. Then suddenly the letter held all her attention. The publishers were very sympathetic towards her illness, but they sent their regrets that her new project must be given to someone else, since it was urgently needed.

Alison sat stunned for a while. She had worked and worked, building up a reputation for herself and taking on as much work as possible in order to establish herself. And now it seemed to have slipped through her fingers.

All her efforts had come to nothing.

A Business Proposition

Sue Reynolds' eyes lit up as Judy handed her the newspaper advertisement when she called to have lunch with the two girls. She had been trying to get the most out of every hour of her holiday before she had to return home to her parents in London.

Each day she'd been feeling more and more refreshed, knowing that Dr Millar was beginning to take up the threads of her life again.

Now she was beginning to think that she'd like to stay a little longer among the friends she'd made in Edinburgh, especially since she had no job waiting for her on her return home.

Now as she read the advertisement which Judy had ringed with a ball-point pen, she began to feel excited.

'Oh, Dr Millar, it's just the sort of thing I used to do at the lab.'

'That's what caught my attention, Sue,' Judy told her, 'but I didn't know whether you'd be interested . . . '

'Oh, I am!' Sue exclaimed. Her face fell for a moment. 'I'd need a reference, though.'

Her eyes were anxious again as they met Judy's, then the older girl smiled.

'I'm sure Dr Rutherford will give you a reference,' she said gently. 'And if a word from me would be helpful, then you shall have it.'

Tears rushed to Sue's eyes. 'You've been so kind to me,' she murmured gratefully.

'I'm a kind person,' Judy said teasingly. 'It's all right, Sue. I know you'll never make the same mistake again.

'The advertisement says you must apply for a form to fill in, so you can telephone on Monday morning, and have it sent here if you like.'

Sue nodded. 'I'll have to find other accommodation if I stay any longer. I can't afford my room at the hotel after next week.'

'Some of our friends next door might help,' Alison remarked, as she finished preparing the lunch.

'That would be marvellous, Mrs Drummond,' said Sue, her eyes shining.

'I think you'd better call me Alison . . .'

' . . . and Judy. We aren't counting grey hairs yet,' Judy joked.

They all laughed and sat down to eat the meal which Judy had cooked. Though Alison's appetite had deserted her, she knew that Judy had gone to a lot of trouble so she did her best to eat her lamb chop and a small helping of vegetables.

Judy watched her rather absently, putting down her quietness and lack of appetite to lethargy after her illness, but Alison's thoughts were miles away.

Suppose she could not now find other work? She'd had a great deal of appreciation for some of the work she had already done, but she couldn't live on past glory.

'Can't you even manage some raspberry mousse?' Judy was asking.

Alison pulled herself out of her thoughts. 'Mousse? No, thank you, Judy. I'm sure Sue will eat an extra helping for me.' She smiled at the young girl.

'You're trying to ruin my figure,' Sue returned teasingly.

All three laughed, and Judy thought how nice it was to see Sue Reynolds so happy and confident again. She had not enjoyed seeing the girl punishing herself with guilt as she had done. Now it was good that she had the confidence to pull Alison's leg.

But Alison's smile had faded quite quickly and once again Judy looked speculatively at her friend. Was something bothering Alison, she wondered.

'I'll help with the washing up,' Sue was saying, 'then I really must go. I'll have to get in touch with my mother if I'm staying a little while longer.'

'Will she mind?' Judy asked.

Sue laughed and shook her head.

'She likes us to be as independent as possible. She'll approve if I try for this job. Oh, won't it be wonderful if I get it?'

'I think you've got a very good chance of it,' Judy said gently.

★ ★ ★

Sue had been gone such a short time that Alison thought she must have forgotten something when the bell shrilled a short time later. This time, however, it was Ken who stood on the doorstep.

'Oh — I thought it was Sue,' Alison remarked, stepping back in surprise.

Ken took a quick look in the hall mirror. 'No, I'm not pretty enough,' he told her with a grin.

'You said it!' Judy said, smiling at Alison as she joined them in the hallway.

'Will you be staying a little while, Ken? Perhaps you could keep Alison company while I do some shopping.'

'Shopping?' Alison asked. 'Have we run short of anything, Judy? Where's my handbag?'

'No — for myself,' Judy said, blushing a little. 'I — I want to experiment with some new make-up, if you must know.'

'Oh — sorry,' Alison said, laughing at herself. 'I didn't mean to be nosy.'

But she was pleased when she saw Judy pause in the doorway and wave to her nonchalantly, just as she used to do. Then her smile faded as she led Ken through to a seat by the fireside where Judy had quickly put down a tray of tea and biscuits.

'Judy thinks I need to be fed every hour,' she told Ken, 'even if it's only tea and biscuits. Is this strong enough for you?'

'Stir it up!' Ken commanded. 'I'll have the second cup. That weak tea would please Sue more than me.'

Alison's eyes darkened and she busied herself with the tea tray. Ken never seemed to be able to resist talking about Sue Reynolds these days.

She was aware of his scrutiny, but she couldn't meet his eyes since her own were slowly filling with tears.

She remembered how constrained she had been when Judy remarked that Ken was falling in love with her. She had not wanted to hear such a thing because she dared not search her own heart.

Instead she had concentrated on her work. Now Ken was beginning to admire Sue and — and it was much too late . . .

'Tears, Alison?' Ken was asking very gently. 'What's the matter?'

His hand covered hers so that it trembled, then she pulled away and searched for her publisher's letter. She didn't want Ken to feel sorry for her.

'I'm sorry to be such a fool,' she said in a matter-of-fact voice, and after a quick wipe with her handkerchief to dispel the tears, she managed to turn to Ken. 'I've had a letter.'

'A letter!' Ken cried, and for a moment it seemed almost as though he were disappointed. 'What sort of a letter?'

'From my publishers,' Alison replied wearily. 'I — I haven't shown it to anyone, but you'd better see it, Ken.'

There was a long silence while he read and re-read the publisher's letter.

'You're worried because you've lost your contract,' he said finally. 'Is that such a tragedy, Alison? Surely you can get others.'

'I got Judy to turn down all my other enquiries when I was ill,' she said. 'Perhaps I can find others, but it will all take time.' She sighed.

'Now, Alison, you know that if you find things difficult, you must come to me,' he told her, a look of sympathy on his pleasant face.

'No!' she cried. He must not feel that he had a responsibility towards her any longer. He must feel free to get on with his own life.

'Is it such a blow to your pride to

allow me to help?' he asked, almost coolly.

'Oh, Ken, no, but — but I mustn't continue to be so dependent on you.'

'At least promise me that you won't worry about it for now,' he asked her. 'Though judging by this piece of cake, you and Judy will be eating for a few more days at least.'

In spite of herself, Alison smiled through her tears. 'We won't starve.' She took up his joke.

'Good, because I actually came round to see if you would like to go to a concert on the eighteenth? It's the Scottish National Orchestra and the programme looks good — Beethoven, mainly, but there's also William Walton . . .'

'I hope you won't mind if I refuse, Ken,' she said tiredly. 'I — I'd rather not go out just yet.'

'It would do you good,' he persisted.

'No, Ken, I'd rather not,' she said, and again the bleak look was back in his eyes. 'I — I have a headache,' she explained. 'I'm not very good company, am I?'

'I'd better go and leave you to rest,' he said reluctantly.

'Perhaps that would be best,' she agreed sadly, and with a few more words urging her to stop worrying, Ken rose and reached for his coat.

'I'll let myself out,' he said. 'See you again, Alison.'

'Cheerio, Ken,' she said. 'It was nice of you to come.'

But as she carried her tea tray into the kitchen, Alison's tears flowed again, and she cried because her heart was sore. She wanted Ken back again, but she didn't want him to stay just because he felt sorry for her.

She wanted him to see her as a friend — an independent woman . . . Someone, perhaps, who was a little bit attractive, even.

Alison looked at her reddened eyes and nose in the kitchen mirror and thought about Sue, who was so bright and vivacious, and another tear rolled down her cheek.

Then quickly she went into the bathroom and washed her face as she heard Judy's key in the door.

'Hello!' Judy cried, breezily. 'Has Ken gone? What did he want, or was it just an ordinary visit?'

'He wanted me to go to a concert on the eighteenth,' Alison said dejectedly, 'but I don't feel like it.'

Judy looked at her woebegone face, and wanted to ask all sorts of questions. Instead she held her tongue.

'Do you feel like telling me how my new make-up looks?' she asked. 'I'll go and slap it on now.'

From somewhere Alison managed a smile. 'OK, put it on,' she said, 'and let's see how glamorous you can look.'

★ ★ ★

That evening Alison again went to bed early, leaving Judy watching a play on TV, but when she was left to herself, Judy's thoughts turned once again to

Malcolm Neill, and what he had said about her mother's first reaction to the scars on her face.

Had her mother been truly upset on her account, Judy wondered. Was Mr Neill right? If so, then she had turned against her mother needlessly. She had loved her mother all her life, how could that love be so easily destroyed?

She realised then that her mother still loved her as much as she ever had and Judy still loved her.

Suddenly she switched off the TV and went over to the telephone to dial her own home. For a while she could hear it ringing at the other end, and she almost hung up, then Mrs Millar picked up the telephone and Judy could hear the slightly fatigued note in her voice as she answered.

'Hello, Mummy, it's me — Judy,' she said, as she had done so often in the old days.

There was a small intake of breath.

'Judy, darling! How are you?' Mrs Millar's voice was uncertain, and Judy felt her heart go out to her. She was beginning to see how much her mother might have suffered.

'I'm fine,' she said gaily. 'I'm sorry I didn't phone before, it was thoughtless of me. You must have been so worried.'

'Oh, that doesn't matter, love. It's just good to hear you now.'

'But, Mum, I've treated you so badly . . . I've been stupid and selfish.' Her voice broke. 'I'm sorry.'

'Say no more about it.' Her mother sighed. 'We've hurt each other, but now I'm pleased to hear you're feeling better. I'm sure Dad will be, too.

'Anyway, what've you been up to in Edinburgh?' she continued, more cheerfully this time.

'You'll never guess,' Judy responded. 'I'm having my portrait painted . . . '

'You're — what, dear? Did you say — portrait painted?'

'Yes, Mum. It's a long story, but Malcolm Neill, the portrait painter, is doing it.'

'But — but he's very famous!' Mrs

Millar exclaimed, almost doubtfully.

'I know. He's a wonderful artist. I know he'll make a marvellous portrait of me. I shall arrange for you and Dad to see it when it's finished.'

'Then — you really feel better, Judy?' Mrs Millar asked.

'A great deal better. I bought some new make-up today and I'm experimenting with it. I'll try to come home soon, and you can see what you think of it. Only, well — Alison has been a little off-colour. She fell and injured her knee, but she's OK again now.'

'Oh, poor Alison. You must give her our love, Judy.'

'Of course I will. Any news?'

'Not a great deal, I'm afraid, though . . . '

Again there was a pause.

'Yes?' Judy asked.

'I had a nice postcard from Blair, dear. It was from British Columbia this time, and shows lovely scenes of Beaver Lake Park in Northern Vancouver Island. Apparently he's gone there for a short vacation with friends, though he hopes to go back to Alaska soon. He's certainly well travelled, isn't he?'

'Yes, he is,' Judy said, her voice more subdued.

'I expect I'm telling you things you know already,' Mrs Millar said, with a laugh. 'Your father says to tell Alison that he has just bought a magazine with her illustration in it, and it's lovely.'

'I'll tell her,' Judy said mechanically.

'Come and see us soon, dear,' Mrs Millar said eagerly.

'I will, Mum, truly I will,' Judy agreed. ' 'Bye for now, Mum.'

'Bye, love.'

Judy hung up the phone and slowly walked towards Alison's bedroom, wondering if she were awake or if she'd dropped off to sleep. She could cheer Alison up with her father's message.

Before lying down, Alison had allowed Judy to read her publisher's letter. She was realising just how much Alison was taking it to heart — much more than she would have guessed.

She paused for a long moment at Alison's bedroom door, then stole on past. She would have liked to have talked to her about her mother's postcard from Blair. He had found time to write to her parents but there had been no postcard or letter for her.

Not that she minded, Judy told herself. Blair was quite free to do as he wished. But it would have been nice to hear . . .

For the rest of the week Judy found herself thinking more and more about Blair, although by Friday the thought of another sitting with Malcolm Neill cheered her up, and she set off once again with a lighter heart.

For a while she hesitated over her new make-up. Ought she to apply it, or would Mr Neill expect to see her looking the same for every sitting?

After a moment she decided that she would apply the make-up. It could be washed off if it was out of place, and she was beginning to enjoy it since it diminished the marks on her face almost to nil, and she really did look like the lovely unfinished portrait of Lorna Neill.

Alison's slight look of surprise, followed by sincere admiration, did much for Judy's ego as she set out once again on the now familiar route to Mr Neill's studio. Once again he was pleased to see her and this time there was a look almost of recognition in his eyes.

'You — you look so well, Judy,' he said, as he welcomed her in. 'You gave me quite . . . ' He paused for a moment.

'A shock?' she asked. 'I'm sorry, I didn't realise. I know that my new make-up makes quite a difference.'

'It does indeed,' Malcolm Neill said, with a catch in his voice.

* * *

Judy chattered happily about things in general as she took up her pose, but for a long time Malcolm Neill found it

267

difficult to get into the swing of his painting. He found Judy Millar's presence very disturbing.

He no longer saw her as a girl who looked like Lorna. Now he was beginning to see her as a glowing girl who was quite unique in herself. She made him feel alive, instead of the old man he had felt he was becoming.

As she talked he was gradually loosening up, then suddenly it was as though something outside himself had taken control of his hands, and he was painting with speed and enthusiasm.

' . . . my ex-fiancé, Blair Walker,' Judy was saying.

'I beg your pardon, Judy.' Malcolm Neill was brought back to reality. 'What about your ex-fiancé? Why ex-fiancé? What happened?'

Judy was silent for a moment.

'I — I suppose I couldn't quite believe he would want to marry me after the accident,' she said.

'Not want to marry you!' cried Mr Neill. 'Did he really treat you like that?'

'Oh, no!' cried Judy. 'It wasn't like that at all. Blair seemed to treat it all as though — as though nothing had happened.

'I broke off our engagement without telling him why at first. I just didn't want to face him. But he persisted in seeing me and, when he did, he kept brushing it all aside, as though it didn't matter.'

'Perhaps it didn't matter to him,' Mr Neill said in his usual abstracted voice as he worked steadily.

Judy was silent, thinking about it. 'But it must have done. I looked different. I *was* different.'

'You look different today from last week,' Mr Neill remarked mildly. 'You are even wearing a different dress, but I believe you are the same Judy inside. Only your outer covering is different. Isn't that how Blair might look at it?' He paused.

'Surely it's significant that he brushed all your protests aside after you had received the plastic surgery. All

269

right — so you might look a little different. But it made no difference to him — and you sent him away?'

'Yes, I did!' Judy sighed. 'Perhaps — perhaps I had to be sure myself . . . '

Mr Neill nodded, then continued gently.

'But although it's good to spend a little time making up your mind, sometimes time isn't always on your side. Lorna and I had so little time together. If she had spent it making up her mind, we would have had no time at all.'

'Yes, I see what you mean,' Judy replied thoughtfully.

When he finally laid aside his brush, he offered to make her a cup of coffee.

'It might taste a little of paint and turpentine,' he added, wiping his fingers on a rag. 'My coffee often does, I'm afraid.'

'This time it won't,' Judy said, grinning. 'If you show me the kitchen, I'll make it.'

Malcolm Neill nodded. He had kept

Judy much longer than he intended, he realised, glancing at the clock, and he admitted to himself that he was loth to part with her. But as she rattled the cups on to a tray, Malcolm Neill studied the portrait which was coming to life under his skilful fingers.

Yes, it was all there again, he thought, with inward excitement. It was all coming back. He had been trying some other work recently, too, and even that was improving. He felt alive and competent for the first time in years!

★　★　★

Judy was in fine spirits when she returned to the flat, though she frowned a little when she found Alison sitting by a fire which was all but dead.

'You've nearly lost the fire, Alison,' she accused her. 'The air is quite chilly.'

'I know.' Alison yawned.

'Well, if you had, you would have had the sharp edge of my tongue,' Judy said, and Alison blinked. 'Do you know how

271

long it took me to get the beastly thing started this morning?'

Judy placed more sticks and coals on the fire, and wafted the flames into life. 'If I didn't love an open fire, I would have given it up long ago and persuaded you to go electric,' she complained in a disgruntled voice.

'I — I'm sorry,' Alison apologised, and Judy threw herself down beside her on the settee.

'I'm the one to be sorry!' She grinned. 'But you're trying my patience, Alison. You aren't pulling yourself round at all. You need to get out more! Why don't you go to that concert with Ken? There are bound to be plenty of tickets, and he may have bought two already. He's going to look in tomorrow. Why not tell him then?'

Alison sat up, looking rather brighter.

'Do you think I should, Judy?' she asked. 'Well — I do feel a little better, so perhaps I will.'

'Good for you,' Judy approved warmly.

Alison was even brighter the following afternoon when Ken called, bearing a picture frame under his arm.

'What have you got there?' she asked, smiling.

'A sample picture frame — size sample, that is. I've just had a great idea, Alison. Why don't you paint a series of pictures, just this size, for me to hang in the shop, and I can sell them for you and deduct a small commission?' he suggested. 'I could easily frame them, you know. It would be good business for both of us.'

Alison's dark eyes began to come alive. She wanted to get back to work again, but she had learned her lesson. She would take it easy this time.

'What sort of pictures?' she asked cautiously.

'Wild-life — landscapes — sea-scapes — whatever you like . . . Even still life, perhaps, but it had better have general appeal. You can think about it, if you like.'

Alison began to smile. She didn't

have to think about it. It would be wonderful to have something to do again and she would celebrate by going to the concert with Ken.

'I don't have to think about it,' she began. 'I . . .'

'Splendid!' Ken cried, his eyes alight. 'Oh, we've got a visitor,' he said as the doorbell rang.

'I'll get it,' Judy said, her own heart light as she saw what Ken had done for Alison.

A moment later Sue Reynolds almost danced into the room. Alison had found her a charming bedsitting-room nearby and Sue was now a constant visitor.

'I've just had a letter,' Sue cried, waving it in the air. 'It came by the afternoon post. I've got that job.'

'Oh, congratulations!' Judy cried, while Alison moved forward to offer her good wishes, and Ken brought up the rear.

'Does this mean that you'll now settle down in Edinburgh?' he asked Sue.

'Yes, and it also means that I'll be in Edinburgh on the eighteenth,' Sue said, her eyes shining. 'So I can go to that concert after all!'

Decisions Must Be Made

Judy's eyes were very bright as she turned from Sue to Ken Doig.

'Why, that's marvellous,' she cried eagerly, assuming that now both Alison and Sue would be going to the concert with Ken.

'It certainly is,' he agreed warmly.

'Because Alison . . . ' Judy broke off as she caught sight of Alison's face. The other girl had an almost agonised look in her eyes and she was shaking her head.

Judy paused for a moment. She had been about to mention to Ken that Alison had changed her mind and could now go to the concert after all, but it seemed that Alison did not want her to say anything.

'Where's that bottle of wine we bought last New Year?' she continued.

Alison found the bottle while Judy

collected four glasses.

'I hope the job is a great success for you, Sue,' Alison toasted the girl.

'And that your new paintings will be equally successful for you, Alison,' Ken said as he turned to her. 'I've a feeling they'll be a great asset to me.'

Alison nodded, though her smile was beginning to waver a little as Judy picked up the sample frame and tried it against the wall.

Then Ken picked up the frame. 'I'll leave this with you then, Alison, if that's all right,' he said.

'That's fine,' she agreed, and smiled brightly as Ken helped Sue into her coat and Judy saw them out of the door.

Alison was sitting in her favourite chair by the fireside when Judy returned.

'What was that all about?' she demanded. 'I thought you said you'd go to that concert with Ken after all. You only had to say and he'd have been delighted to book another ticket, but instead you were glaring at me and daring me to say one word!'

'Oh, Judy!' Alison sounded tired. 'Surely it was obvious why I didn't want to say anything. Ken had asked Sue to go, and she must have been unable to accept because she was leaving Edinburgh. So he asked me.'

She shrugged.

'But now that Sue's staying after all — well, everything's OK. I'm certainly not going to play gooseberry.'

'Play gooseberry!' Judy cried. 'Don't be ridiculous! Ken's just being nice to Sue — that's why he's taking her about. You must see that. It would have given him a lot of pleasure if you'd agreed to go. You can't believe Ken prefers Sue!'

Alison turned on her rather angrily.

'Judy, please,' she said tiredly. 'I — I just don't want to discuss it. Ken's quite free to go where he pleases and with whoever he wants to. It has nothing to do with me.' Her voice cracked and she turned away and quickly switched on the television.

Judy sat in silence, completely taken aback as she realised that Alison was taking this very much to heart. She had never given any sign of caring for Ken, but the fact that he was taking out another girl was obviously going deep. And Judy could see Alison had no intentions of discussing it with her.

Judy sat for a long time while Alison stared at the television screen, apparently absorbed in a programme which had never appealed to her before, then Judy rose and collected the wine glasses.

'I'd better put these away,' she said awkwardly. 'Do you fancy a cup of tea?'

Alison's dark eyes were luminous, then she smiled. 'Thanks, Judy. I'd love a cup of tea.'

Alison spent a long time that night trying to come to terms with herself. It wasn't going to be easy to stop herself from running to Ken whenever she needed his support, but she knew she'd have to do it.

She'd also have to make a worthwhile

job of the pictures he'd asked her to paint, and the following morning found her back at her drawing board.

The weeks of idleness had taken their toll, she thought. Her fingers again felt stiff and awkward, and although the ideas were coming alive for her they fell far short of the work she was accustomed to turning out.

★ ★ ★

She was scrapping her first effort when Judy walked in with the shopping, and stopped for a moment when she saw what was happening.

'Oh, Alison,' she said, with sympathy. 'Isn't it going well?'

'No, that was hopeless.' Alison replied. 'But I half expected it. I've got to get myself worked in again.

'Ken suggests twenty-four pictures, so I thought I'd do six each of say — flowers, birds, landscapes and the sort of picture which would look appealing in a child's bedroom. You know the sort of thing . . . '

She did a few swift strokes and Judy found herself looking at a small, plump child feeding a few fluffy chickens. It seemed amazing that it had appeared so quickly.

'Oh, how pretty!' Judy cried.

'Yes — it's pretty enough, I suppose, but I'm having a job to give it all a bit of style. I've tried a few drawings this morning and I'm afraid they just look, well, pretty.'

'Nothing wrong with that, I'm sure,' Judy said. 'Anyway, I'll leave you to get on with it, Alison. I've made an appointment at the hairdresser's for a trim. Next time I might pluck up the courage to have it cut short again.'

'I used to like your hair when you wore it short,' Alison encouraged her, pleased to see that Judy no longer felt the need to hide behind her hair.

Her friend was looking in the mirror. Not so long ago she'd have been turning away and allowing her longer hair to come forward over her face.

Now, however, she was pulling it back from her face to see the effect.

Alison's thoughts turned once again to Ken and she sighed a little as she began to map out her first really serious effort at painting the pictures he required.

Slowly it took shape under her slender fingers and, after she'd rested her chin on her hands and gazed at it for some time, she decided it would do.

Judy's trip to the hairdresser's had been good for her morale. Now, however, her thoughts turned to Blair Walker as she looked at herself in the mirror. She became more subdued.

Soon it would be spring again and she was remembering a previous spring when they went for long walks together and planned a future which held nothing but promise and delight.

Judy's eyes dulled as she realised how badly those plans had gone wrong, and how much of it might have been her own fault.

She remembered Blair's voice insisting that her appearance made no difference to him, but she hadn't listened. She had considered her own feelings all the time. She had never once wondered how he felt, yet with only a few words Malcolm Neill had made her see things from Blair's point of view.

She must have hurt him very much, Judy thought rather painfully. And now he had gone out of her life. She was beginning to rebuild her life without him and no doubt he was also living a good life in North America.

Judy thought about the happiness in her mother's voice when she had rung up and put things right between them. That happiness had found a warm echo in her own heart.

If only she had the opportunity to apologise to Blair in the same way — suddenly his forgiveness was very important to her. How could she let him know she was no longer embittered and unhappy, she asked herself.

Her new clothes, make-up and hairstyle made a different woman of her, but people changed in any case as they grew older. Blair would have changed, too, and it wouldn't have mattered to her.

That evening Judy spent some time writing a friendly letter to him, mentioning how pleased her mother was to receive his postcard.

Perhaps in a week or two she would receive an answer. Her heart beat a little faster at the thought.

'I'm just going out to post this letter,' she called to Alison.

'OK,' Alison replied absently. Her efforts had tired her and she was still looking critically at the picture when Judy returned with Ken in tow.

'How's it going, Alison?' he asked.

She looked up at him quickly then turned away, swallowing painfully as he bent over her.

'I — I'm not very happy with it, Ken,' she said. 'There's more work to do on it yet, but . . . '

'But it's the very thing,' Ken said, taking the picture over to the window. 'It's colourful and . . .'

'Pretty,' Judy and Alison said together, so that they both laughed.

'What's wrong with that?' Ken asked. 'It would look well in anyone's sitting-room, and that's what we want, Alison. At least, that's what's suitable for my shop. I know what will appeal to my customers.'

'Yes, I know, Ken,' Alison said gently, 'and that's what I've tried to do, only . . . I feel I could do better work for you. I just don't know what's the matter.'

'You're too pernickety.' Ken grinned. 'I don't think you can improve on this one all that much, and you can't spend too much time on it either, otherwise they'll cost too much, won't they? Keep them simple.'

Alison nodded. She was learning about a new form of commercial art.

★   ★   ★

'How was the concert?' she asked. 'Did Sue enjoy it?'

'We both did,' Ken said. 'I think you might have enjoyed it, too, Alison.'

'Oh, I'm sure Sue made you a — a charming companion, Ken,' she said quickly, as she bent down to pick up a tube of paint.

Ken looked at her averted face and his eyes sobered.

'Of course,' he said quietly. 'Let me know then, Alison, when I can come and collect the pictures. I'd better come in the car.'

'OK, Ken.' She nodded. 'I'll do that.'

The days seemed to pass slowly for Judy and she was first out each morning to collect the mail, but there was no familiar air letter from Blair, and she gradually had to force down her disappointment.

When she called for her sitting with Mr Neill one Friday, he could see that her laughter and high spirits were slightly forced. Yet she was looking quite lovely, he thought, as he took her coat.

'This one is almost finished now,' Mr Neill declared, as he began to put the highlights into her hair.

'What will you do with it?' Judy asked.

There was no reply for a moment.

'I mean, would my parents be able to see it?'

'Oh, I should think so,' Mr Neill said absently, now that the work had caught hold of him.

'You've got lots more canvases stacked about,' Judy observed.

'I'm doing better work now,' Mr Neill said with satisfaction. 'No, my dear, you've moved your head a little . . . That's better . . . '

'Sorry,' Judy said, and was silent for a moment. 'My friend, Alison, is very dissatisfied with her work at the moment, too. She's doing some popular paintings and a friend is hoping to sell them in his shop.'

Judy found herself telling Mr Neill about Alison, and he listened with his usual interest, which seemed casual, until he asked a pertinent question, showing her how well he understood. Hearing about Alison, he seemed to understand very well indeed.

'Where are the pictures being exhibited?' he asked.

'Ken Doig's stationery shop,' she explained, 'but I rather think they are just going up on the wall to be sold like any other picture. I mean, it isn't an exhibition, as such.'

'I see,' Mr Neill said thoughtfully. He paused for a moment and stood back to look at the portrait. It was a study in gold and silver and it glowed as though the canvas was filled with light. From amidst the brightness, the girl's face shone in beauty and serenity.

Mr Neill felt a catch at his heart. It was the finest piece of work he had ever done.

'Have you pocketed your pride and written to your young man?' he asked gently, and Judy coloured.

'You knew I would, didn't you?'

'I hoped you might.' He looked directly into her face and waited for her to speak.

She was silent for a moment. 'He hasn't replied,' she said at last.

'Surely there's time. Alaska is a long way away.'

'Yes, but — but there's been time. I think Blair must be thinking very carefully about whether he wants to write to me or not. I — I must have hurt him very much.'

'We all hurt one another from time to time,' Mr Neill said quietly. 'That's what makes us human. My Lorna wasn't really a saint and neither am I. Saints must be hard to live with.'

Judy laughed at his rueful tone. Mr Neill always made her feel better.

'You'll hear,' he said confidently. And if she did not, he added to himself, then the young man didn't deserve Judy Millar.

Slowly Mr Neill painted, his face very thoughtful.

'We'll still need one or two more

sittings,' he said to Judy. 'I hope that's all right.'

'I enjoy it,' Judy told him happily. 'I've baked a few cakes for our tea. It's on me today.'

She went straight into the kitchen and he could hear her singing softly as she set out the teacups. He would miss her very much when the picture was completely finished.

* * *

Alison worked hard after she got into the swing of doing the pictures, though she felt there was nothing of herself in them.

Ken, however, was delighted with the finished work, and was happy to ring her up when he made their first sale.

'You'll make your fortune in no time,' he told her, and she laughed.

'Oh, I'll settle for bread and butter.'

'Alison, if you . . . ' Ken began but she cut him short.

'Sue's just been here. She's on her

way round to look at the pictures in the shop. I thought you'd be pleased to see her, Ken.'

There was a short silence. Ken felt that he was being well and truly put in his place.

'I'll be quite pleased to see Sue,' he said quietly. 'Cheerio, Alison.'

She hung up the phone and rested her head in her hands. Judy was in her bedroom having a rest, just when Alison would have been glad of her company.

It was an hour later when a tall, distinguished gentleman with grey hair mounted the stairs to the flat and rang the bell.

'Good afternoon. I'm Malcolm Neill,' he told Alison when she opened the door.

Her eyes widened. 'Oh, Mr Neill — do come in,' she invited. 'I'll just fetch Judy. She's having a rest.'

'No, no. Actually, I rather wanted to talk to you, Mrs Drummond,' he said as he sat down by the fireside.

'I've just been to have a look at your

paintings in Ken Doig's.'

'Oh!' Alison's face coloured rosily. She felt very embarrassed that an artist of Mr Neill's standing had been to look at her pictures.

'They aren't very good, are they?' she asked. 'I don't know what it is, but — but I can't give them that extra touch. I can't explain . . . '

'You don't have to,' Mr Neill said, smiling. 'I spent several years in 'No Man's Land' after my wife died. It's only recently — since Dr Millar allowed me to paint her — that I've got that important little quality back again; that thing you can't explain.'

Alison sat down, her eyes warm. How nice it was that Mr Neill understood. 'I don't know what to do,' she confessed. 'The pictures are selling, too, yet it's so unsatisfying somehow.'

Mr Neill nodded. 'I know exactly what you mean. Have you any other work you can let me see, Mrs Drummond?'

'Not really,' she confessed. 'Only

odds and ends — things I've toyed with in between projects.'

'I'd like to see those,' Mr Neill said firmly, and she went over to her large art cupboard and pulled open a deep drawer, lifting out drawings and paintings on canvas.

The artist examined them all very carefully, carrying them to the light and occasionally running his fingers over them. He selected a charming little painting of a child and raised his eyebrows.

'A neighbour's child,' Alison said. 'They moved away before I could finish it. This is a street scene, from my window here. I — I did it when I was rather troubled.'

'Yes, I can see that.' There was power in the picture which seemed to give real, vibrant lines to the hurrying crowds.

'I'm exhibiting at the Venetian Galleries for one of their summer exhibitions,' he said.

'The Venetian Galleries!' Alison

exclaimed with awe.

It was a name to bring interest to the eyes of any artist, since the galleries were world famous.

'I'll have space for two more pictures,' he said, 'and I would be happy to exhibit two of yours, Mrs Drummond. Would you paint them for me?'

Alison gasped and sat down abruptly. 'I — I couldn't!' she cried. 'I'm just not good enough.'

'I think you are,' Mr Neill said matter of factly.

'But you — you've seen the ones in Ken's shop!' she remonstrated.

'You weren't stretched,' he said gently. 'You painted your boredom into those pictures. Now I'm asking you to give everything you've got, and then some more. I know you have the talent to do this.'

He smiled down at the girl.

'Six pictures such as that street scene from the window and the wonder in a child's eyes.'

'I don't know what to say.' Alison looked at him steadily.

'You would prefer to think about it?' he asked sympathetically.

She ran her tongue over her lips and looked up at him.

'I'll do it,' she said bravely.

'Good girl. There's still plenty of time, but I need hardly say . . . ' He paused and she nodded with understanding.

'I'll set to work straightaway, Mr Neill.' Alison could feel the familiar tingling of her fingertips which told her she would be able to do what was required of her. 'I won't let you down!'

'Good for you, Mrs Drummond. I'll see you again, so it's au revoir.'

'Au revoir.' She smiled, then leaned back against the door after he'd gone. If she did this work, then she'd have very little time to work on Ken's pictures, she remembered, and she had given the promise to Mr Neill.

Ken might not be very pleased with her when he found out.

Ken took Alison's news with the quiet acceptance which was customary of him. Sue had arrived with him, saying how pleased she was with the picture she'd bought. It was an impressive painting of Edinburgh Castle — one of Alison's landscapes.

'I've been round it all three times now,' Sue said. 'I've been to most places, but I've really fallen in love with the Castle! I adore the view from up there, but best of all I adore the sense of history. Somehow I hadn't thought it existed outside London.'

'Outside London!' hooted Judy. 'Such ignorance, Sue Reynolds.'

'All right, all right,' Sue cried, putting her hands over her head. 'Ken has already put me to shame a few times. It's all lovely, though, and I can't wait for the Festival when it comes round.'

'You're forgiven.' Alison smiled. Sue's enthusiasm warmed her.

But now Sue was voicing her

disappointment that Alison wasn't continuing to paint more pictures of the Castle for Ken.

'I can't really explain, Ken,' she said awkwardly. 'This exhibition for Mr Neill will mean that I have to give more of myself. It won't be easy. I must have time on my side.'

'Is it that important to you, Alison?' he asked, glancing at her.

She nodded, but didn't look at him. He mustn't see that it was a great deal less important to her than Ken himself.

'What about income?' he asked, always practical. 'Would you allow me to buy all the pictures you've done for me, en bloc?'

'Oh no, Ken, that wasn't the arrangement,' she protested, then saw that he was looking hurt. 'Well . . . '

'I can sell them,' he told her briskly. 'You're quite determined to be independent, aren't you, Alison?'

She said nothing but she knew he was displeased. She was going to find it difficult to keep his friendship.

★ ★ ★

On Friday Judy returned from Mr Neill's studio with light footsteps.

'I had a quick peep at my portrait today, Alison,' she said. 'Mr Neill says it's going to be the centrepiece for his exhibition at the Venetian Galleries. Isn't that exciting?'

'Very exciting,' Alison said. Her fingers were sticky with nerves and so far her efforts were not going well for the exhibition. She'd been about to go and see Ian Thomson regarding new canvases which would need to be stretched on to boards, when Judy walked in.

'Plain biscuits today,' Alison said. 'We're budgeting.'

'I know,' Judy said. 'As a matter of fact, I've been wondering about going back to work. I even dropped a short note to Charles Rutherford. Just a friendly note, I mean . . . '

'Judy! Not yet, surely. I thought it would take at least a year.'

'I know,' Judy said, 'but I really do feel better now. I've got back most of my confidence.'

'Most?' Alison repeated, a question in her voice.

Judy said nothing. All her confidence would have come back if only she'd heard from Blair. But she'd heard nothing, and secretly she was very hurt. He could surely have managed an ordinary, friendly letter, she thought.

The following afternoon she and Alison were delighted when the bell rang and they opened the door to Dr Rutherford.

'Charles!' cried Judy, and received a warm hug from the tall man who stood on the step.

'One for Alison, too,' he said, and Alison was lifted up like a leaf and whirled round. 'Well, it's good to see you two girls again. My word, Judy, you do look better! Not that you weren't all right before . . . ' he added hastily, while Judy collapsed with laughter.

'You're still the same,' she said

breathlessly. 'Always ready to put your foot in it, but I know what you mean. There was room for improvement, and I don't think I've done too badly.'

'You certainly haven't,' he agreed, 'And what about you, Alison?' You look pale. You've been working too hard.'

'She's going to be a famous artist,' Judy said proudly. 'She's exhibiting with Malcolm Neill at the Venetian!'

'Well!' Charles said, eyeing Alison with new respect.

'Oh, Judy!' Alison cried, blushing.

'How long can you stay? Are you on holiday?' asked Judy.

'Only for a long weekend. I have to travel back on Monday but I had to come and see what Edinburgh has that I haven't. I seem to be losing all my staff to the place. I had to give Sue Reynolds a reference.'

'She's very happy here, Charles,' Judy said. 'You'll see her later. Tell us about the lab. Who's working where and on what project?'

Alison left them talking shop for a

little while. She was delighted to see Charles Rutherford again, and to see Judy so cheerful and natural with him.

'We're re-organising everything, Judy,' Charles said. 'Adele Mason wants to stay on permanently, but I want to know your plans if you have any. I'm rather hoping you can tell me how you feel about coming back, before Monday.'

'That quickly?' Judy asked.

'Well, I thought I'd tell you straight-away so that you can think about it,' Charles said. 'But you're certainly looking very fit. Miracles have been worked. It looks as though you've quite a lot to tell me.'

The bell shrilled and Judy began to rise.

'I'll go,' Alison called, and hurried to open the door.

A moment later Judy heard her small exclamation of surprise, then the deep tones which were all too familiar to her.

Her face went very pale as Blair Walker walked into the room.

No Longer Afraid

Judy leapt to her feet as Blair walked towards her with outstretched hands.

For a long moment it seemed as though they were the only two people in the room, then Judy became aware that Alison and Charles were also welcoming Blair excitedly.

'What a lovely surprise!' Alison cried. 'When did you get home, Blair?'

'I got leave a few days ago,' he said almost absently, his eyes on Judy's face.

How well she's looking, he thought, and how wonderful to see her grey eyes so bright and happy again.

Alison was asking Blair if he could stay for dinner, but he shook his head, smiling.

'I wanted to ask Judy if she'd come out with me,' he said, turning back to her. 'I really want to talk to you, Judy.'

'I'd love to,' she said, then turned to

look awkwardly at Charles and Alison. 'If you two don't mind, that is.'

Alison smiled at her gently.

'We don't mind at all, do we, Charles?'

Judy hardly waited for Charles Rutherford's reply before rushing into her bedroom and looking out her prettiest outfit.

Just as well I've started to take an interest in clothes again, she thought, as she slipped into a warm, green suit.

Her cheeks were glowing with excitement and all three stared at her with admiration when she returned to the drawing-room to find them talking together.

'I'm ready,' she said to Blair, and together they walked out into the cool of a beautiful evening.

'I thought we could book a table for dinner,' Blair said, as he took her arm. 'That would give us time to have a stroll in the Princes Street Gardens. How does that sound?'

'Just fine,' Judy agreed happily,

waiting while Blair hurried into one of their favourite hotels. When he returned they entered the park.

'I came as soon as I got your letter, Judy,' he told her. 'I've been moving about quite a lot and the letter had been following me! I wondered — hoped — it meant you'd changed your mind.'

'Oh, Blair, I'm so glad to see you again,' Judy said, her eyes shining. 'When I didn't hear from you, I began to think you didn't want to — to be friends any more. Anyway, I know now how much I must have hurt you.'

'I've never stopped loving you,' Blair said, taking her into his arms. 'You must know that your accident made no difference to me at all.'

'I know that now, but at the time, I — I couldn't bear for you to see me.'

'Oh, Judy darling,' Blair whispered. 'To me you're more beautiful than ever.'

He slipped a hand into his pocket and brought out a small jewellery box containing her engagement ring.

'Will you wear it again, Judy?'

'Yes,' she whispered, and her eyes sparkled with tears of joy. 'Oh, Blair, I'm so happy — even more than I was before!'

Blair drew her into his arms, holding her close as he kissed her with all the desire he had felt for her over the months of waiting.

'It's been a long time, my darling,' he murmured softly.

'A very long time,' Judy agreed. 'Sometimes I thought I'd never see you again.'

'Oh, you'd have seen me again,' Blair assured her. 'Even without that precious letter, I'd planned to come back and try again. You wouldn't have been rid of me so easily!'

⋆　⋆　⋆

Over dinner, Blair told Judy about his life in Alaska.

'I still have two or three months to

305

do, then I have the option of staying on permanently or coming home. Could we be married very soon, Judy, then you can come with me?'

He smiled tenderly.

'It would be like a long honeymoon for us. After that we'll decide what we want to do, whether we want to travel or settle down.'

His eyes were bright as they looked into hers.

'Either way, I'm not going to let you out of my sight until we're married. Do you think you could arrange that at short notice?'

'My mother could,' Judy said, her eyes shining. 'And all this speed might prevent her from inviting half of the county! She won't want it too quiet, though, love.'

Her eyes shadowed a little.

'I hurt my parents, too, Blair, but perhaps this will make it up to them.'

'We mustn't disappoint your mother,' said Blair, 'I'll go along with whatever she wants to do.'

'Let's go home and tell Alison,' Judy said, after they had discussed every aspect of their future together. 'All the same, perhaps we ought to telephone our parents first of all. Oh, and I'll have to tell Charles Rutherford. He wanted me to go back to the laboratory!'

Blair looked at her curiously.

'I'd have thought that would be the last place you'd want to go!'

Judy laughed.

'I'd have gone back if you hadn't come home, Blair, but now I'm quite glad I don't have to. You see, I really have put it all behind me. Even the lab holds no fears for me.'

Blair held her close in his arms again and kissed her as they walked back to the flat.

'We have all our happiness in front of us,' he said.

* * *

Alison was still up when they returned to the flat and she hurried to congratulate both of them as soon as she saw their shining faces.

'No need to ask what has happened,' she said. 'It's pretty obvious, just from looking at you.'

'We're hoping to be married in three weeks' time, Alison.' Judy said, 'so I can return to Alaska with Blair. You'll be matron of honour, of course.'

'Just try asking anyone else!' Alison said.

'I'll have to go through to Calderlea on Monday,' Judy went on, 'to help Mother with the preparations. I — I suppose you wouldn't be able to come with me, Alison?'

Alison bit her lip. She was finding it very difficult to do the high-quality work which was essential for the two pictures Mr Neill had commissioned. Although she had a few weeks in hand, she couldn't afford to waste time.

'If you don't mind, I'd prefer to leave it for a week or two, Judy,' she said. 'Anyway, if I know your mother, there won't be a great deal for me to do, and we can soon get together over what you'd like me to wear.'

'I'll probably be travelling up and down from Calderlea anyway,' Judy promised. 'I mustn't let Mr Neill down for a start. Thank goodness the portrait is almost finished.'

'Oh, by the way,' Alison said, 'Charles Rutherford has invited all of us to lunch at his hotel tomorrow, and that includes you, Blair, and Sue Reynolds.'

A short time later, Judy went to the door to see Blair away then returned to dance round the room.

'Oh, Alison, I'm so happy,' she said, and Alison's eyes were misty as she took in her friend's obvious happiness.

She could not trust herself to speak.

The following morning Judy slept rather late, having been so excited it had taken her a long time to drift into sleep.

Alison gave her breakfast in bed.

'Oh dear, I am being pampered,' she protested.

'Well, we're in no hurry,' Alison said.

'We're all meeting Charles at his hotel at one o'clock, so we've a long morning ahead of us. I'll be popping out for a while, if that's OK.'

Judy listened to the soothing music of church bells.

'Are you going to church?' she asked, knowing that Alison rarely missed Sunday service.

'No, I'll go this evening,' she replied. 'I — just wanted a word with Ian.'

'Well, don't get too bogged down talking shop,' Judy warned. 'And don't forget our lunch date! It will probably be my last chance of seeing Charles before he goes back to London, and I want to thank him for his concern for me and all his help. He's a good friend.'

'There was a time when I wondered if he wasn't a little more than that,' Alison admitted, and Judy looked surprised.

'There's never been anyone for me but Blair,' she said, and Alison's eyes were sad for a long moment.

'Yes, I know what you mean,' she said.

'Things change though, Alison. We have to keep adjusting our lives to circumstances.'

Alison sighed and thought about the pictures for Mr Neill, which were giving her so many problems.

Her first instinct had been to talk to Ken, then she remembered she had promised herself that Ken should be free to live his own life without bothering about her.

So her thoughts had then turned to Ian. He would understand her problems, Alison decided, as she hurried along to the art shop.

Ian was delighted to see Alison. 'I've got your canvas ready for you,' he assured her.

'I'll need another one, Ian, but there's no hurry. I'm still stuck on the sketches for my first picture. Mr Neill mentioned a street scene and as he talked about it I felt I could almost see what he was driving at. But now — now

I just can't make it come alive for myself.'

She sighed deeply.

'I've made one or two attempts, but everything's so flat. I — feel that it isn't going to work, and that I'm just not good enough.'

'Calm down, Alison,' Ian said briskly, detecting a note of near panic in her voice. 'You've got plenty of time to experiment yet, surely?'

'Longer than I usually take,' Alison admitted, 'but Mr Neill made me see this was going to be really challenging, Ian. It can't be turned out quickly.'

She shrugged despondently.

'If these pictures are going to mean anything I'll have to put a tremendous amount of thought and effort into them. Oh, Ian, I'm sure I'm not good enough.'

Ian looked down at Alison's bent head, his eyes filled with sympathy.

At one time he'd have longed to put his arms round her and comfort her, but he had come to realise that

Alison wasn't for him.

Now he came to sit down beside her.

'I've known Malcolm Neill for years,' he said gently, 'and believe me, he wouldn't have asked you to paint those pictures if he hadn't been sure you're good enough.'

'I'm afraid of letting him down,' Alison confessed. 'I'm afraid my work won't be up to his standards.'

'Don't you think other artists might feel the same?' Ian asked. 'Look, Alison, I have two complimentary tickets for an exhibition at the Venetian Galleries next week. How about coming with me and having a look at what other artists have done?'

Alison's eyes brightened. 'That sounds terrific, Ian. I'd love to go.'

'OK — I'll call for you on Wednesday afternoon,' he said. 'We'll go then.'

It was a merry party who met at lunch, and Judy and Blair were showered with congratulations over their forthcoming wedding.

'You *will* wear white, won't you?' Sue

pleaded, with stardust in her eyes. 'Don't go wearing simple things like a plain suit just because you're arranging it all at short notice. It must be a fairy-tale wedding.'

'I'm going to wear my kilt,' Blair said. 'What about you, Charles?'

'Oh, definitely my kilt!' Charles agreed, to a great deal of laughter.

'Well, Ken will have to join the clan, too!' Sue put in. 'He'll look very good in the kilt.'

Alison's gaze dropped and Charles Rutherford looked at her thoughtfully. She was rather more subdued than he liked, and as he turned to look at Sue, he saw that she was also regarding Alison thoughtfully.

'I hope you'll find time to have tea with me occasionally after Judy goes, Alison,' Sue said. 'I'm going to be lonely.'

Alison smiled.

'I can't imagine you being lonely for long, Sue, but I'll be glad to see you, of course.'

'Unless she decides to come back to London,' Charles put in. 'I'll have to start offering inducements to my staff!'

'Well, I'm certainly gaining experience, Dr Rutherford,' Sue said. It was funny, she thought, but seeing her old boss again had made her feel slightly homesick.

She might think carefully about how long she would stay in Edinburgh. Besides, it would be nice to see her parents again . . .

* * *

Alison looked forward to her outing with Ian the following Wednesday. It was quiet in the flat now that Judy had gone home, though she was glad of the peace for a little while.

News of Judy's engagement had leaked out and they had been surprised by the number of friends and neighbours who had called to wish her well. Ken had been especially delighted for her.

He had brought her a lovely piece of silver as a wedding gift.

'My word, but things can happen fast,' he said as he looked around at the cases which Judy had decided to take home. 'You're going to be left on your own again, Alison.'

Her eyes sobered at his words. She hadn't wanted to think too deeply about how much she would miss Judy.

'I'll just have to get used to it,' she told Ken. 'I can't lean on — on Judy all my life.'

'No, you can't,' Ken agreed gently.

Alison spent the following two days doing sketches for her pictures and answering the door, so she was happy when Ian called for her on Wednesday in his car.

'We should have booked for the theatre instead of an art exhibition,' he said, when he saw her. 'You look fabulous, Alison.'

'No, I'm really looking forward to seeing this exhibition,' she assured him, getting into the car as Ian held the door open for her.

'Ken Doig said he thought you would be when I mentioned I was taking you,' remarked Ian cheerfully, as he guided the car through the busy traffic and into the quieter streets where the distinguished Venetian Gallery was located.

Ian found the tickets, and escorted Alison up the broad marble steps to the hushed gallery.

'It's all so beautiful,' she whispered. 'But it's a bit awesome.'

'Well, it isn't for beginners,' Ian agreed. 'But then, you aren't exactly a beginner yourself, Alison. I wonder if you've stopped to consider just how much experience you have now.'

'Well, I don't know if I'm ready for all this, yet,' Alison said, as Ian escorted her into a long, well-lit gallery, with polished parquet flooring. Two men were exhibiting — one a sculptor and the other an artist who specialised in seascapes.

Alison enjoyed looking at the sculpture since every piece was a work of art which appealed to her without her having to analyse exactly why. She looked at the reclining figure of a mother playing with a young child and smiled.

'That's charming, isn't it?'

'Yes, it is,' Ian agreed. He waited patiently until Alison turned to the pictures, but this time she was silent as she walked round.

The artist had painted the sea in all its moods, sometimes reflecting magnificent sunsets and sometimes the sea gently lapping against a holiday beach. Alison studied each one intently, in turn, then went back to look at them all once more.

'I can see the mood behind each one,' she said, 'and the technique is very interesting.'

'Is it beyond you?' Ian asked softly.

She shook her head after a while.

'No.' she admitted honestly. There could be no false modesty between her and Ian. 'No, I think I could paint just as well as this. In fact, I know I could.'

'So, you aren't afraid of the place any more?'

She turned and smiled, almost with relief.

'No, I'm not afraid. Thanks for bringing me, Ian. I'm sure I can tackle it all much better now.'

'That's my girl!' he said. 'Look, how about having tea with me before I take you home? I'd appreciate your advice on what to buy Judy for a wedding gift. In fact, I thought about a piece of that sculpture until I looked at the prices!'

'I know.' Alison laughed. 'You'd have to be a millionaire!'

'So I decided on a good old-fashioned clock,' Ian went on. 'Should we choose one on the way home?'

'Yes, I'd love to help,' Alison said. 'You've made me feel a lot better today, Ian.'

'I'll settle for that.' He chuckled.

Over the next two weeks Alison worked very hard, though she had to put her paintings aside when Judy rushed back from Calderlea every few days to do more shopping and make more arrangements.

She had chosen a beautiful wedding gown which was sure to please Sue.

Alison's dress was on simpler lines in sea-green silk, but it brought out the beauty of her fair hair and dark eyes.

'Oh, Alison, you look stunning in that,' Judy said when Alison tried it on at home. 'You won't be short of admirers.'

'Oh, no-one will notice me! They'll be too busy looking at you!' Alison told her. 'Aren't you due for your final sitting with Mr Neill today?'

'I should be on my way now,' Judy told her, looking at her watch.

Malcolm Neill's eyes filled with pleasure when Judy arrived, though deep in his heart was a twinge of sadness that it was for the last time.

But he owed to her the fact that he was full of vigour and life, and he could only rejoice with her in her own new-found happiness as he put the final touches into the picture.

'What are your plans for after the wedding, Judy?' he asked.

'Blair and I are flying to Alaska. It will be like a glorious honeymoon for me, though Blair has to finish his project there. After that, we'll come home before Blair starts another project — wherever it might be.'

Mr Neill painted a few more strokes. 'Then you'll be back for the exhibition?' he asked.

'Of course. We mustn't miss that,' Judy said, her eyes bright. 'Besides seeing your other pictures and Alison's, I'm thrilled that my portrait is going to be exhibited. My parents are so very proud that you've painted it. Will it really be finished today?'

'The actual painting is finished now, but it has to dry out and, of course, I'll have to spray it with re-touching varnish before framing. It can be varnished again at a later date.'

He smiled.

'All that takes time, but don't worry, it will be ready for the exhibition.' He was silent for a moment. 'Judy, I — I'd like to give you the portrait as a wedding gift,' he said unexpectedly.

Judy was taken aback by his offer.

'Oh, Mr Neill! But — but it must be valuable! I mean, all your work is very valuable . . . '

'I couldn't put a price tag on this work,' Mr Neill said gently. 'As I explained already, it broke the deadlock in me and enabled me to do work which is deeply satisfying. I hope you understand, Judy.'

'It will be our greatest treasure.' Judy said, her voice deep with emotion. 'I — I feel I owe you my happiness. You made me realise I could be myself again, if only I tried a little harder.'

When Judy walked away from the studio that day. Malcolm Neill looked after her from the doorway until she was out of sight. Then he sighed a little as he returned to the studio and lifted the portrait into a corner to dry.

It was the end of a chapter, but the

beginning of a new life for both of them.

★ ★ ★

Mrs Millar was delighted to welcome Alison to Calderlea a few days before the wedding, though she had left very little for Alison to do.

'You're far too thin, my dear,' she chided. 'I can see I'll have to feed you up again.'

Alison laughed. 'I won't get into my lovely dress if you do that!' she protested. 'Oh, it's good to be home again.'

Mrs Millar's eyes were gentle as they rested on the girl. Alison had described Calderlea as 'home' almost involuntarily.

She was delighted to have both her girls home again, but whereas Judy was glowing, Alison looked as though she could do with a little bit of mothering.

Mrs Millar, herself, looked happy and contented, Alison thought. The slightly-anxious expression she had been wearing on the last occasion was now gone, and she was her old self again.

'We've managed to book a hotel reception even at such short notice,' she said to Alison with satisfaction.

'Yes, and the numbers have been growing every day,' Judy put in, 'until the manager dug his heels in! But I don't think Mum can find anyone else to invite.'

'Well,' Mrs Millar looked slightly abashed, 'it isn't every day your only daughter gets married.'

'I hope it only happens once!' Judy laughed, then bit her lip a little as she glanced at Alison. If only she could find happiness again, Judy thought, then my own would be twice as precious.

Blair, too, seemed to be caught up in wedding arrangements and they had seen little of one another over the past week. But she could wait, thought Judy, contentedly.

The long, anxious days when she'd

thought she had lost him had taught her true values and patience. Her happiness was all the greater now that it was appreciated so much.

Judy's wedding day dawned clear and bright and the whole of Calderlea seemed to come alive for the event. The church was packed to capacity while many local people crowded round the door to see the guests arriving.

The hotel was fully booked with guests from London and friends from Judy's college days, and there seemed to be a steady stream of traffic from Edinburgh and Aberdeen as friends and relatives of both Judy and Blair arrived.

Ken Doig had brought Sue in his car and Ian had picked up Mr Neill, who was looking very smart and distinguished for the occasion.

Charles Rutherford had booked in at the hotel and was enjoying another visit to Calderlea and meeting Judy's parents once again.

After the tiring days of preparation, it was Judy and Mrs Millar who were most nervous on the morning of the wedding, and Alison who had to be the mainstay.

Judy felt that her new make-up looked unnatural and garish and for a moment her eyes were anguished. Then Alison took charge and helped to calm her down and put things in perspective.

'It's only because you're nervous,' she said. 'Just take it easy and let me smooth your face cream in for you. Blend it out at the corners . . . There, that's better. Anyway, Blair won't care if you don't put any on at all!'

'No, I don't suppose he will,' Judy said, smiling at last.

Mrs Millar was suddenly quite sure she had forgotten something very important, but couldn't think what it was. Patiently Alison ticked off every detail, and the older woman, too, began to relax.

'So all that's left is a hat for you,' Alison said at length, her eyes dancing teasingly. 'That's what you've forgotten!'

They all laughed because the first thing Mrs Millar had bought was a delicious concoction of lavender flowers and feathers. She had tried it on several times since.

Judy looked so beautiful in her bridal gown that she brought a few appreciative gasps from the congregation as she walked up the aisle on her father's arm.

Blair's love was shining in his eyes as she walked forward to stand beside him and to listen to the beautiful words of the marriage ceremony.

Alison felt a lump in her throat as she took Judy's bouquet. She hadn't been to a wedding since she lost Alec and now her own wedding ceremony came back to her with vivid clarity.

Tears stung her eyes as she listened to Judy and Blair making those selfsame vows that she and Alec had, and she sent up a silent prayer that their happiness would be more lasting than hers had been.

The best man was a doctor friend of Blair's whose wife and baby daughter were in the congregation. Alison walked out of the church on his arm and posed for photographs while a great many people looked on admiringly at the bride and 'groom.

Judy's nerves had completely vanished and Blair held on to her hand as though she might vanish out of his sight.

★　★　★

But Alison was aware that Mrs Millar was now beginning to react to all the excitement.

Although the older woman was enjoying the wedding reception and joining in the general merriment, she was beginning to feel the strain of the long months of Judy's illness and to realise she was finally parting with her daughter.

Alison had seen her wiping away a tear now and again and she took the opportunity of giving the older woman's hand a reassuring squeeze when everyone crowded into a reception room at the hotel.

'I'm so happy for them — really I am,' Mrs Millar murmured.

'I know.' Alison smiled gently.

'But I'll miss her,' Mrs Millar went on. 'It's different now that everything has been cleared up between us. At one time I was too hurt to cry, but now I can shed a few tears because I'm so happy. It's a funny old world, isn't it?'

Alison stood aside for a little while as friends and relatives were greeted by the young couple who received their congratulations.

She turned to find Sue Reynolds beside her and complimented Sue on her lovely maroon velvet suit and lacy cream blouse.

'Well, if you can't dress up at weddings,' Sue said, 'when *can* you dress up? It's such a lovely occasion. When I get married, I intend to dress like a queen.'

'I'm sure you'll look beautiful, Sue, whatever you wear,' Alison told her.

But she spoke absently, her emotions still jangled by everything that had happened to her that day.

Suddenly she felt a hand on her arm and she turned to find Ken looking at her. There was no humour in Ken's eyes.

'Hasn't it been a lovely wedding?' she asked too brightly.

'Well, Judy deserves a beautiful wedding,' Ken agreed. 'Anyway, I've been wanting to speak to you, Alison. You used to turn to me if you wanted any help, but now you just don't come to me at all.'

His expression was grave.

'Instead you've been going to Ian Thomson. I'd just like to know why you've turned against me.'

With Courage And Love

For a moment Ken's words hardly registered with Alison as she turned to stare at him. His face was white and there was an angry look about him which mingled with the hurt in his eyes.

A few yards away, Sue Reynolds had been speaking to Ian Thomson and now she turned casually to look for Ken, who had been escorting her round the reception.

Alison felt her own anger rising as she turned back to him.

'I just can't understand you, Ken,' she said coldly. 'Why should I always be running to you with my troubles? In any case. I don't really want to discuss it.'

Her cheeks were flushed and her eyes glinted as Ken looked down at her.

'But, Alison, you must know . . . ' he began, but already she could see Mrs

Millar beckoning to her. Judy would have to go soon to change into her 'going away' clothes and Alison had promised to help her.

'Please don't bother me, Ken,' she said almost brusquely. 'I'm very busy just now.'

'Then there's no more to be said.' Ken shrugged as he stepped back to let her pass.

'That's right,' she agreed, deliberately looking in Mrs Millar's direction.

He turned away when Sue came up to greet him once more, while Alison quickly followed Mrs Millar. She felt really annoyed with Ken.

He and Sue had obviously been enjoying every moment of the wedding, yet the only time he had found to chat to Alison had been spent criticising her.

Again Alison had to force back the tears. It had been a tiring day for her emotionally but now she must put all her own thoughts and feelings behind her and help Judy prepare for her honeymoon.

The young couple were spending one or two days at an unknown destination before flying to Alaska.

Quietly, Alison helped Judy to change.

'Take one more look at a fairy-tale princess before I help you to take off your wedding dress,' she said to Judy, turning her to the mirror. 'It's such a lovely dress — you looked wonderful in it.'

'Thanks, Alison.' Judy sighed. 'Let's hope Blair will like me in my going-away outfit.'

'Today Blair would like you in old slacks and a sweater!' She laughed. 'Don't you worry, he'll be very proud of you in this. Look, you've got a hook caught in your hair, so stand still while I fix it.'

Suddenly the girls' eyes met in the mirror and Judy's filled with tears.

'Oh, Alison, I owe you such a lot,' she whispered. 'If only you could be happy, too.'

'I am happy, love,' Alison assured her.

'And in case you've forgotten, you're the one who helped me to get over losing Alec, so we've really helped one another, you and I.'

'I — I'll miss you,' Judy said.

Alison nodded. 'I know, but think how happy you are now that you have Blair. So no more tears!'

'Oh, they're happy tears,' Judy said, smiling as she reached for a tissue.

As she spoke, the door opened again and Mrs Millar came in. Alison looked from mother to daughter then slipped out quietly and left them alone for a few moments.

Soon, however, there was a great deal of noise and happy laughter as the young couple left in Blair's car, which had been decorated with streamers and old tin cans.

'We'll have to stop at the first dustbin,' he said ruefully, while his best man reminded him of what his car had been like when the positions were reversed.

Mr and Mrs Millar, along with

Blair's parents, waved them away, then Alison went to slip her hand into Judy's mother's, feeling the older woman's fingers clutching her own.

'Try to stay for a day or two, Alison,' said Mrs Millar.

'I'll stay,' Alison promised. 'It's been a lovely wedding, hasn't it?'

Mrs Millar sighed. 'Yes, it has. I'm so thankful everything has turned out right for Judy at last.'

Alison nodded. She didn't want to dwell on how much she would miss Judy.

That night, however, as Alison crawled wearily into bed, her thoughts were all with Ken Doig. Once again she was seeing that hurt expression in his eyes as he asked her why she had turned against him.

And once more she could hear her own brusque, angry words as she told him not to bother her. Alison's heart was heavy with regret. How could she have been so abrupt with Ken!

She thought about the many times he

had helped and advised her, and all she had given him in return was a thoughtless rebuff.

Alison felt heartsick at the thought of it, and she knew she would have to apologise to Ken after she returned home. But would he accept her apology?

★   ★   ★

For the next day or two, Alison was kept very busy helping Mrs Millar to cut up the wedding cake and pack away Judy's wedding gifts for safe keeping.

Mr and Mrs Millar had invited Charles Rutherford round for a meal before he returned to London, and he had accepted very happily.

'I'm going to miss Judy,' he said ruefully. 'Blair has just married my best specialist in her own particular field, though no doubt Dr Mason will turn out to be equally good one day.'

'Judy got her interest from her grandfather,' Mrs Millar put in.

'Walter's father, that is.'

'Yes, it skipped a generation in me.' Mr Millar laughed.

'Young Sue Reynolds may be returning to London in two or three months,' Charles said musingly. 'We're re-organising and there could well be an opening for her then. That would give her time to complete the work she's doing at the moment.'

'But — she's so happy in Edinburgh,' Alison said. 'I thought she might actually settle there.'

'She'll be happy again in London, too,' Charles said, his eyes gentle as they rested on her. 'She seems to have come to terms with herself.'

The following evening Mrs Millar answered a telephone call, then shouted for her husband excitedly.

'It's Judy and Blair,' she cried. 'They're on their way to Prestwick now after touring the Highlands. Their plane leaves tomorrow and they wonder if we'd like to go and see them off. Oh, Walter . . .'

'Well, why not?' Walter Millar asked, his arm round his wife. 'We can take Alison.'

But as Alison took the telephone receiver for a few, cheerful words with the happy couple, she decided she would leave that send-off to Judy's and Blair's parents.

The time would pass and very soon Judy and Blair would be home again for the summer exhibition at the Venetian Galleries. In the meantime she had a great deal of work to do.

Nevertheless, as she travelled back to Edinburgh, alone for the first time in many months, Alison experienced a sense of true loneliness. How empty the flat would be!

She had been learning to live on her own when Judy came to stay with her, but the flat would seem twice as empty now that Judy had gone.

Still, it would help her concentrate on her work again, Alison consoled herself, though she knew that wasn't strictly true. Judy had always been there to criticise and encourage her, and Alison had often produced better work because she knew Judy's opinion would be an honest one. Now there would be no-one.

Slowly, she climbed the stairs to the flat and looked in her handbag for her key. The spare key was once again being kept by Ian Thomson and, even as she searched, Alison began to wonder if she had mislaid her own.

With a sigh of relief she found it in her purse and opened the door, expecting to feel the usual rush of cold, slightly damp air.

But the flat was warm and cheerful, and as she walked into the drawing-room she saw that a fire was burning brightly and the small table she and Judy had kept for cosy occasions was set nearby.

★　★　★

A moment later, Ken Doig walked out of the kitchen. His brown eyes looked anxious and pleading as he smiled at her, a trifle uncertainly.

'I hope you don't mind, Alison,' he said. 'I know you — you more or less said I was to mind my own business, but I didn't like to think of you returning to an empty flat.'

He smiled again.

'So I borrowed the key from Ian and I've lit the fire and cooked a meal for both of us. Nothing fancy, mind — just a grill with a few things I know you like. Oh, and I've brought you some flowers to brighten the place up. I've put them in that vase . . . '

Alison looked at Ken's less-than-artistic arrangement of chrysanthemums, which were sticking upright like soldiers out of a narrow vase.

Somehow it was the last straw.

'Oh, Ken, Ken . . . ' she whispered. Then she was sobbing helplessly while he came and put his arms round her.

'Have I been too pushy, Alison?' he asked. 'I didn't mean . . . '

'No — you just don't know how grateful I am,' she said through her tears. 'I was expecting to come home to — well, nothing. Now it feels as though I've really come home.'

'All your homecomings could be happy, Alison,' Ken murmured as he held her close. 'You must know I love you, darling, and that I want you to marry me.'

He stroked her hair tenderly.

'You wouldn't ever be lonely again, I'd make sure of that. There's nothing I wouldn't do for you, Alison.'

For a moment she stayed quietly in his arms then she gently pushed him away.

'Oh, Ken, please don't ask me to make that decision just yet,' she pleaded. 'It's still too soon after Alec's death and I — I, well, Judy's wedding sparked off some old memories. That's why . . . Oh, Ken, I'm so sorry for the way I spoke to you.'

'No, I'm the one who should apologise,' Ken said quietly. 'I was so jealous of Ian. I thought you were turning to him.'

'And I thought you might want to live your own life, Ken, without having me hanging round your neck,' she said.

She almost mentioned Sue, but bit back the words. It was clear to her now that Ken and Sue were no more than very good friends.

'I thought it was time I stood on my own feet,' she went on softly.

'But all I want from life is you,' he insisted. 'Alison, is there any hope for me?'

This time she nodded, her eyes very bright.

'Of course, Ken, so long as you don't rush me. I must be absolutely sure. I — I couldn't bear it if anything went wrong.'

He kissed her tenderly, his heart well content.

'That's all I ask, Alison, just the chance to show you there are a great many happy years ahead for both of us. We can start whenever you feel ready to share your days with me.'

His expression grew serious.

'I know how precious your years with Alec were to you and I wouldn't want to belittle those memories.' He groaned. 'I'm not making this very clear, am I? Do you know what I'm trying to say?'

'Yes, I know — and, Ken, I was very lonely when I thought I'd lost your friendship. I'm glad you're here.'

His arms grew tight around her. Suddenly there was a hissing from the kitchen.

'Oh, my goodness, it's my meal!' Ken cried, while Alison began to laugh as he switched off the grill and did a repair job on his sausage and bacon.

'I'm so hungry now I won't mind a bit of, well, extra crispness round the edges,' Alison said cheerfully.

'It looks as though that's exactly what you'll get,' Ken said ruefully. 'I'm sorry, love.'

'Never mind,' she said, her heart light as air. 'By the way, your flowers are just beautiful.'

* ★ ★

Malcolm Neill's summer exhibition at the Venetian Galleries was a great occasion.

Alison had managed to settle down to painting steadily and, encouraged by Ken and sometimes by Ian Thomson, she began to capture the charm of her Edinburgh street scene.

Mr Neill had taught her not to be afraid of colour and to paint what she saw and felt. So, taking his advice, she worked hard, until one morning she put her brush aside with a feeling of deep satisfaction.

The second picture was finished, and although she felt almost exhausted by her efforts, there was an underlying elation. She had accomplished something of which she could be proud.

Ian's praise was voluble when he came to look at the picture. Ken on the other hand said very little, but Alison knew that, of the two men, Ken was the more deeply moved.

'I can't really tell you how much I like it, Alison,' he said. 'I don't think I could put it into words. I hope I don't have to.'

'No, the look on your face is the finest praise I'll have, Ken,' she told him.

Ten days before the opening of the exhibition Judy and Blair flew home again from Alaska, and Alison travelled up to Calderlea for a family reunion.

Judy looked wonderful and was filled with a new-found confidence.

'Blair's going back to Aberdeen for a year or two,' she told Alison, 'and we've been looking at a house which might suit us very well.'

'She wants only a wall to hang that portrait on,' Blair teased.

'And fireside chairs for our parents,' Judy said, laughing. 'Not to mention Alison and Ken.'

'It's open house, in other words,' Alison said happily. It did her heart good to see Judy so happy.

The exhibition opened to a blaze of

publicity and there was a great deal of interest aroused as the visitors studied the pictures painted by Alison Drummond, whose name was becoming more and more well known.

Mr Neill was obviously very proud of his protégée as she and Ken Doig walked hand in hand round the exhibition.

But pride of place was given to the truly magnificent portrait of Dr Judy Walker.

Mr and Mrs Millar stood for a long time gazing at their daughter's portrait, their hearts full when they looked at Judy's loveliness.

Malcolm Neill had wandered round the exhibition, entirely satisfied with the success of his work. He had listened to the critics and he passed on their praise to Alison.

'You've done something really worthwhile, Mrs Drummond,' he said. 'You've painted life as it really is — and it can be wonderful if you face it with courage — and love.'

The words seemed to ring in Alison's ears as Ken's hand closed over hers. Then Judy and Blair came to stand beside them.

Together, the four young people would face life with courage and love.

THE END

Jane Carrick is a pseudonym
of Mary Cummins who also writes
as Mary Jane Warmington.

We do hope that you have enjoyed reading this large print book.

Did you know that all of our titles are available for purchase?

We publish a wide range of high quality large print books including:
Romances, Mysteries, Classics
General Fiction
Non Fiction and Westerns

Special interest titles available in large print are:
The Little Oxford Dictionary
Music Book, Song Book
Hymn Book, Service Book

Also available from us courtesy of Oxford University Press:
Young Readers' Dictionary
(large print edition)
Young Readers' Thesaurus
(large print edition)

For further information or a free brochure, please contact us at:
Ulverscroft Large Print Books Ltd.,
The Green, Bradgate Road, Anstey,
Leicester, LE7 7FU, England.
Tel: (00 44) **0116 236 4325**
Fax: (00 44) **0116 234 0205**

Other titles in the
Linford Romance Library:

THREE TALL TAMARISKS

Christine Briscomb

Joanna Baxter flies from Sydney to run her parents' small farm in the Adelaide Hills while they recover from a road accident. But after crossing swords with Riley Kemp, life is anything but uneventful. Gradually she discovers that Riley's passionate nature and quirky sense of humour are capturing her emotions, but a magical day spent with him on the coast comes to an abrupt end when the elegant Greta intervenes. Did Riley love Greta after all?

SUMMER IN HANOVER SQUARE

Charlotte Grey

The impoverished Margaret Lambart is suddenly flung into all the glitter of the Season in Regency London. Suspected by her godmother's nephew, the influential Marquis St. George, of being merely a common adventuress, she has, nevertheless, a brilliant success, and attracts the attentions of the young Duke of Oxford. However, when the Marquis discovers that Margaret is far from wanting a husband he finds he has to revise his estimate of her true worth.

CONFLICT OF HEARTS

Gillian Kaye

Somerset, at the end of World War I: Daniel Holley, unhappily married to an ailing wife and father of four grown-up children, is attracted to beautiful schoolteacher Harriet Bray, but he knows his love is hopeless. Daniel's only daughter, Amy, who dreams of becoming a milliner and is caught up in her love for young bank clerk John Tottle, looks on as the drama of Daniel and Harriet's fate and happiness gradually unfolds.

THE SOLDIER'S WOMAN

Freda M. Long

When Lieutenant Alain d'Albert was deserted by his girlfriend, a replacement was at hand in the shape of Christina Calvi, whose yearning for respectability through marriage did not quite coincide with her profession as a soldier's woman. Christina's obsessive love for Alain was not returned. The handsome hussar married an heiress and banished the soldier's woman from his life. But Christina was unswerving in the pursuit of her dream and Alain found his resistance weakening . . .

THE TENDER DECEPTION

Laura Rose

When Sophia Barton was taken from Curton Workhouse to be a scullery-maid at Perriman Court, her future looked bleak. Was it really an act of Providence that persuaded Lady Perriman to adopt her as her ward? Sophia was brought up together with the Perriman children, and before sailing with his regiment for India, George, the heir to the title, declared his love. But tragedy hit the family and Sophia found herself caught up in a web of mystery and intrigue.